CW00860259
THE
LAST
FOREST
PARALLEL
STREAMS
VOL 1
Alexander Way-B
Daisy-B

ISBN 978-1-7398885-2-7
Published in the UK

Louannvee Publishing
www.louannveepublishing.co.uk

Dedicated to my mother, who never stopped believing in me – telling me to aim at the seemingly impossible with determination!

To Thomas Daulton
For having the patience and enthusiasm to help me turn a story into a book and the honesty to always challenge every detail of my plot!

For Daisy-B, my bookworm daughter, for all your wonderful ideas and help making such a wild tale together!
Keep dreaming and being lost in books and imagination!

And especially for every unlikely heroine and hero out there – wherever you are!

The fire in a slightly oversized hearth flickered inside a cosy rural room. The orange light danced around the walls, playing chase with the shadows. Beside the fire in a rustic rocking chair sat a little old lady. Her curly hair was entirely white. Wrinkles, but especially smile lines, crisscrossed her kind and gentle face. She dozed by the warm fire, with a blanket draped over her legs.

'Hhhhun,' she said as she stirred, and her eyes opened. Her brown eyes glinted in the natural light. Eyes that seemed even older and even wiser than the lady. 'That dream again,' she muttered to herself.

'Oh, Grandma, you are awake,' came the soft voice of a girl sitting looking out of the window on the other side of the room.

'Yes, dear Gelwin,' the old lady said. 'I had that dream again. At least I think it was a dream, or a memory. My muddled mind can't see the difference anymore.'

Gelwin, who had scraggly and untidy hair, scurried over and sat in a chair beside her gran, clutching a small sketchbook. 'Tell me what happened in your dream, Gran,' she said with adoring fascination.

'Oh, my dear, I have told you this dream so many times. Do you not tire of an old lady's silly stories?'

Gelwin sidled up closer and gazed into her gran's eyes. 'No, Gran, I always love to hear about your dreams, or your stories.'

The old lady smiled gently at her granddaughter, her calm voice almost a whisper. 'Very well then, dear. It was the dream about that little girl again. She was so familiar this time.'

'Go on, Gran, tell me from the beginning the story of the girl.'

The old lady smiled. 'It's just a silly dream, but very well, my dear. I don't know if it is her real name, but everyone just calls her Der, which I think is short for Derwin and means dear friend!'

CHAPTER ONE

Der was the kind of girl that never excelled at anything. She was small, weak, and hated by – well, everyone in her world. She had long unkept hair and wore rags for clothing. Her jumpers, T-shirts and jeans all had more holes than a piece of Swiss cheese. They were like a patchwork quilt of repairs and probably contained more new fabric than the original garment. Her best clothing was her school uniform, which was a strange assortment of second-hand garments cobbled together.

Yet despite her neglect, Der was a gentle, yet determined girl. She was the kind of girl that would keep getting up after falling over a hundred times, and with every fall a little more determination would burn in her eyes. But I suppose she had to be, for she lived virtually alone.

When I say virtually, I say that because there was Frank. Her legal guardian, he had been her mum's boyfriend, before her mum had run off with someone else, or so she was told. And her father had never been around. Frank was left with a three-year-old Der, and decided to keep her, as he could claim extra benefits. He was a simple man, who liked to go to the pub every night drinking, come back late drunk and go out early in the morning to work.

Der wasn't sure quite what it was that he did and had never had a conversation lengthy enough with him to ask. He did the bare minimum for her, but he prided himself in reminding her on a daily basis, that if he didn't, she would be living on the streets.

Der spent most of her time in her tiny room. It was the smallest room in the flat, had no carpet; wallpaper that was peeling off; and not even curtains or a lampshade. She slept on an old mattress in a sleeping-bag. And apart from a desk which she had salvaged from a skip about a year ago, she had little furniture of her own. Der had nothing and no one, but she was tough, deep down. She also had a secret, something that no one else except one other knew; and certainly not the galumphing bullies at her school.

It was a Monday morning and the school had put on a 'non uniform' day. They were the days that Der dreaded the most. She awoke early and rolled off her old mattress onto the hard rough floorboards.

She stood up and got dressed. While all the other kids in her school were having lengthy debates with their friends about which set of clothes from their wardrobes they wanted to wear and listening to their friends say things like, 'Oh, yes that sweater really brings out the blue in your eyes!' Der rifled through the few rags she had.

Choice was certainly not on the menu for her. She grabbed a pair of what were once blue jeans, but now covered in repairs. Every here and there was an area of the original denim that peeked its head round from behind a great landscape of patches, just to remind you that they *were* once jeans. She pulled on an old shirt many sizes too big, also patched here and there, and finally an old sweater that was half unravelled. Then she put on three pairs of socks, strategically choosing ones with different placed holes, so that she could cover her toes and feet entirely.

She quietly grabbed her old school bag and crept into the kitchen. Frank was asleep in a heap on the sofa, where he had probably fallen after a heavy night out drinking and watching football with 'da ladz' as he referred to them. His eyes twitched and his flabby face wobbled as he snored. One arm lay flopped on the floor with a half-finished bottle of 'Jake's Triple Strength Head-banger' beer in his hand, which strangely was still upright and not on the carpet.

Next, Der quietly grabbed some bread and jam. She pulled a blanket over Frank and crept out of the front door into the cold morning air. Now the real challenge began, she reminded herself. Wearing an old pair of plimsolls (which were so well worn that there were holes through the soles blocked off with cardboard), she crept down the back stairs of the grey, grimy block of flats. When she got to the bottom, she slowly opened the metal security door and peered out.

Can you imagine what it would be like to be a mouse creeping around a jungle filled with cats and birds and other ferocious predators? Well, that is exactly how she felt.

Der took a few steps to the right and darted across the road. The other side of the road had lots of trees on one side of the pavement and tons of badly parked cars on the other. She wove her way between cars and trees, constantly trying to stay in cover, and constantly peeking behind and down the street.

As she turned one more corner, she took extra care to check the coast was clear, before darting into an alcove behind a bush. She stayed silent and watched lots of expensive trainers and shoes walk past. She knew each pair by now and recognised each voice. She stayed very, very still and silent, waiting for the last set of feet to pass by. Then she waited some more.

Eventually the school bell rang signalling the start of school. She sighed and very slowly emerged from her hiding place, idly walking the last few metres to the gates.

'Late again, Der? That is 365 days straight now!' a stern looking teacher said as she entered, glaring at her over bifocals. 'You are probably the student with the closest address, why do you always come last?'

'Sorry, sir, won't happen again,' Der said in a tone that had a subtle undercurrent of sarcasm. She slowly walked across the yard to the front door of the glass three-storey monstrosity that they called 'Squires Modern Comprehensive'.

The roof sprawled all over the place as if the designer had blown his nose on a hanky and submitted it as the design. But it wasn't the design that disturbed Der the most. Eyesores of modern architecture she could deal with, but the glares and laughter coming from the third-floor class window, her classroom – now that was tough.

She simply smiled back, in defiance at them all and began the ascent to the third floor. Lethargically she strolled down the corridor, knocked on the door and entered. Trying to draw as little attention to herself as she could, she crept round the other blocks of desks and sat down at the back of the class.

A tall kid dressed in the latest fashion and brand new clean white trainers swivelled round and looked Der up and down with a sneer. 'See you wore your best clothes, tramp!'

A snigger broke out around the boy, until Der replied, 'Yeah, but at least my clothes didn't cost the environment, Jack!'

Jack did a double take, then gave Der a nasty look and whispered, 'You will pay for that later, tramp.'

Der was what some people would call 'a glutton for punishment'. She would never just take it, even though she knew that it only made things worse. She wouldn't give them the satisfaction. She knew she could never ever win, but deep inside she had a fiery defiance to never go quietly, and never to simply just submit. A trait that often got her into tons of trouble and had made her the single most picked on kid in the school, the town – hey, maybe even the universe!

'You and whose army, fashion boy?' she replied. Jack swivelled back round and glared at her, his face glowing red from anger.

'Right, kids, turn to page twelve of rudimentary maths,' the fierce teacher bellowed out, cutting down all glances, whispering, and other non-studious behaviour, like a scythe. The kids slowly took an old, dated book from their desks and began to read.

A gruelling two hours later and the whole class were begging for the break to come – all except one: Der. The bell rang, followed by the deafening screech of chairs scraping, and all but one of the kids making a dive for the door and belting down the corridor towards the fresh air outside.

Der snuck a peek around and tipped her pencil case on the floor. She looked down at the spillage with an expression of feigned surprise and crouched down to put them back into her pencil case, one by one. Moving at a pace that would make most sloths proud, she eventually zipped it up, picked up her bag and walked towards the door carefully.

She peered left, then right, then down the corridor. If she could just make it to the toilets, she could avoid trouble. She quickly but quietly fled down the corridor to the left. And just as she turned the corner, mere metres from the loo and a safe cubicle to lock herself inside, she screeched to a halt.

'Here she comes, the garbage queen,' chuckled one of the school's notorious older bullies, Duncan, surrounded by his mates, who were all cackling like hyenas. Before she could turn and run, one of his obedient friends had blocked the corridor behind her – Jane, a tall elegantly dressed girl with long blonde hair. She glowered at Der with spite.

'Going somewhere, Der? What kind of name is that anyway. Was your no-good mother appalled by how stupid you were when you were born and named you 'Derrr', is that why she left you? Is that why she abandoned you? Is it, DERRRRRR?' Jane brought her hand to her eye as if pretending to cry, and the hyenas cackled loudly in a frenzy.

Der felt tears welling up but refused to give them the satisfaction. Instead, she turned and stared at Jane, who stood a full foot taller, square in the eyes and answered sternly. 'My mother was very clever. She was an electrical engineer and she named me Derwin because it was my grandfather's name. At least it is unique – unlike, well, everything about you!'

Jane's face was a mixture of satisfaction that she had found a nerve, and anger at Der's comeback. She stepped towards Der and was about to reply with a double dose of spite, when Duncan, with his slicked-over hair, complete with two lines shaved into the side, stepped forward.

'Where you going, trash bag orphan? We're only just

getting started.' The hyenas cackled again and closed in further.

Der's brain said, 'Just ignore them, it will be easier,' but her mouth bypassed the logic of her grey cells and continued. 'Came to let you know that you shouldn't lie on the grass when your father is mowing the lawn!' The hyenas glared at her, awaiting their alpha's attack.

'What did you say, you hand me down tramp?' Duncan roared as he moved in for the kill, and Jane closed in too in the hope of grabbing her. He towered over Der and pushed her roughly to the ground. Der slowly got back up and put on a smile, despite the pain.

'Thanks for that, do you feel better now?' she said sarcastically. Jane, while still blocking the exit, grabbed Der's bag, wrenching it out of her hands. Der turned to grab it back, but before she knew it, Jane had thrown it to Duncan. They passed it to and fro over Der's head with the rest of the group cheering as she stood watching them, and when they failed to get a reaction they tipped the contents onto the floor.

'Thanks, I needed to give my bag a bit of a sort out,' she said with tons of sarcasm. Just when she had finished putting everything back, Jane made a grab for it again, and tipped it back onto the floor. Der felt tears welling up, but refused to give in.

'Nice! Now that you have mastered that, any other tricks?'

Der said with her hands on her hips. 'You know, I have seen monkeys do smarter tricks than you!' She knelt down and put the things back into her bag again, then looked up at the jeering pack. 'Now while I love hanging out with you lot – watching you pick on someone half your size so that you can feel superior and good about yourselves – I do have things to do you know.'

The group closed in on Der, ready to make the kill. She looked around at them all and realised that she might just have gone too far this time. 'Hi Mrs Hythe!' Der bellowed out. A cold silence fell over them. A name that could strike fear into even the bravest and hardened bully.

Mrs Hythe was a short, wiry lady with a long, pointed nose and large eyes. But make no mistake: what she lacked in size she made up with ferocity. She was the headmistress of the whole school, and she ruled it with an iron fist. Many a rough, tough class clown or bully had been sent to her office, strolling out of the class walking tall, and mere minutes later coming back a ball of blubbering mess, to sink back into their seat, and never give a peep again.

The trick that the more successful bullies had learned to perfect, was avoiding her at all costs. That is why when Der called out her name, a strange panic swept through Duncan, Jane and their motley gang. Eyes began to twitch and they all changed their postures, nervously swivelling round to see where she was.

In that moment of panic, Der made her sly and calculated exit. By the time Duncan and Jane had realised that in fact Mrs Hythe was safely sitting in her office at the other end of the school, sifting through her collection of detention sheets, and not behind them, Der was long gone. And by the time Jane and Duncan had got themselves together, planning a search, it was time for class.

***

Many hours later, the bell echoed along the corridors to signal the end of school, it was followed by an earthquake-like sound of chairs scraping, doors slamming and a great heaving river of kids all pushing and jostling to get outside as quickly as possible. Der was the only one still sitting ten seconds after the bell, and the only one to not share the desire to rush outside. She peered at the board and pretended to copy down the last of the notes in her exercise book.

She tentatively peeped around to see who was left, but the room was empty and even the teacher had scurried off briskly. Der glanced up at the clock and a small cheerful smile appeared on her face, but it wasn't that school was over that made her smile, or the prospect of trying to get home without being caught by the bullies, or even the grand prospect of foraging for food, while avoiding Frank, her sort-of-stepdad. No, it was none of these things: today was a Wednesday, her favourite day of the week, when she would visit her favourite place. It was the one highlight of her week.

She shovelled her things into her bag, then threw it

over her shoulder and left. She checked every corner of every corridor as she went, just in case there were any stragglers, especially of the bully variety. When she crept out of the gates, however, she went in the opposite direction than her home.

After the careful walk, like a mouse crossing a room while a cat slept, she arrived at a small high street. The street looked like it was once a popular seaside tourist destination a long, long time ago, but now most of the shopfronts were boarded up and only a few remained open, hanging on by their fingertips.

She gazed through the dirty smudged windows at the shopkeepers inside and the ageing stock – as she passed each one, the shopkeeper looked up expectantly. Eventually she came to a different type of shop all together.

The building looked just as tired and dishevelled, but inside it was well-lit and filled with all sorts of odd and mundane things. There was old clothing, books, ornaments, furniture, and a whole load of toys.

Der slowed down, turned and pushed the old heavy door open. As it opened it jangled an old-fashioned bell.

She wandered towards the front desk, expecting to see her only friend, Moreen. Moreen was a lady in her 80s, with pure white hair, a round face with rosy cheeks, and always wearing a beautiful floral dress. Der had known her for a few years now and loved to listen to her tell stories about her travelling act in a very different time, now long past.

Every Wednesday this was Der's routine. In her sad and grey world, Moreen was one of the only people she truly enjoyed spending time with. She would pop in after school and Moreen would share a flask of hot sweet tea and homemade fruit cakes. And they would sit together and chat for ages, until the evening came and closing time.

It was also Moreen that had helped nurture Der's secret interest. For every Wednesday on leaving the shop, Moreen would hand Der a bag of broken things. Yes – you read that correctly. And why on earth would anyone want a bag of broken things? Well, I am not going to tell you! Not yet anyway. You will have to keep reading.

Der smiled as she walked through the aisles of second-hand objects, stopping occasionally to look at items. A small white porcelain swan caught her eye, and she delicately picked it up to look, her face filled with delight. After carefully placing it back in the same place she meandered on and eventually came out at the counter.

'Hi Moreen, how was your day?' she grinned, but there was no reply. After some time, an old gentleman appeared, dressed in strange and oddly out of place clothing. Der plucked up the courage and said, 'Is Moreen here?'

The man smiled warmly and gently replied. 'Ah, you must be Derwin! I have been expecting you. Moreen said you would be in today. I am sorry but Moreen isn't at work today. She had something to do, and I am filling in for her. But she left you something. Let me see.'

The old gentleman turned without waiting for Der to reply and began to rummage through things on a shelf at the back. Eventually he gave out a murmur of, 'Ah, here it is.'

He picked up a basket, turned to walk back towards Der, hesitated, then scurried off for a while longer, only to return to Der with the same basket. 'Here you are, Derwin. Moreen has left you a note and a cake in there too.'

Der smiled and said, 'Thank you.' She reached into the basket and pulled out the note. It was written in joined-up swirly writing and read:

'Dear Der, I am sorry, but I had something to do today and could not be with you. I am looking forward to seeing you next week. But for now, here are seven things for you and one of my fruit cakes. Take care, dear, and see you next Wednesday.'

Der smiled and thanked the man, then carefully put each of the items into her bag. When she turned to leave and say goodbye, the man was gone and the shop was empty. She left, quietly closing the door gently behind her and then hurried home full of excitement.

The great grey block of flats was soon looming up in front of her, and she snuck round the back of it to use the stairs. There *were* elevators but they barely worked. Puffing and panting, she emerged from the staircase onto the eighth floor and knocked on Frank's front door.

Most of the kids of her age at school had keys to their homes, but not Der – but then again, most of them had caring parents or guardians too. A banging and clattering came closer to the other side of the door and it swung open.

A tall man with a bald head wearing a tank top covered in a veritable range of stains, of which I would not have time to list here, glared down at her. He had thick black eyebrows, a short stubby nose and a thin cruel mouth.

'Oh, it's you!' were his words, yet contained in them was the sense of burden, disappointment and hindrance.

'Thought it was Fat Al coming for a few drinks before we hit the Squawking Parrot for our main refreshments! Well don't just stand there: go and make yourself scarce,' he said with disdain.

Der scuttled away in the direction of her room. Moments later she heard raucous laughs and enthused voices. Der pushed her bedroom door closed until she heard the gentle click and let out a sigh.

From safely behind the door, she reached into her bag, pulled out the letter from Moreen and unfolded it. Placing it gently on the floor, she pulled out the cake and took a long sniff of it. For you or me, it might just have been a fruit cake, but for Der, she felt the love and attention that her friend had taken to make it for her. It was something that she seldom experienced. She bit into it and smiled. Der thought about her day at school and the cruel kids there and wondered if the whole world was the same.

After she had finished the cake, she scraped the paper cake case with her teeth to get the last bits. Then she reached into her bag and pulled out the items from the shop. She laid them out and looked over the eight items, taking the time to inspect every detail.

Just then something odd dawned on her and she looked back at the letter she had left unfolded on the floor. 'Seven items, it says, not eight!' Der muttered to herself, her eyebrows clashing together in the centre of her forehead.

'That is very odd, her letter *definitely* says seven, but there are definitely eight. Maybe she wrote it in a hurry,' she muttered as her attention reverted back to the broken items she was raring to repair.

She stood up and quietly opened her desk drawer – a task that had a certain knack. She had rescued the desk a while ago, when someone was throwing it out. The drawer had no handle and she had to prise it open in a specific place; an eccentricity that Der had chosen to leave, as it helped to keep nosy Frank out of her most prized things.

She slid her drawer out, removed some school library books on electronics for later, and then lifted the drawer out completely clear of the desk and pulled something from the void beneath where the drawer sat. It was a crudely cobbled-together set of tools inside a half-torn pencil case.

She knelt down near the eight broken objects, opened

the pencil case, and placed each tool on the floorboards. The first object was a small radio. She removed the batteries and then selected a rusty old screwdriver and meticulously opened up the plastic shell of the radio.

She expertly and methodically traced the wires and other items, inspected the circuit board, and for a split second pondered. She checked through the wires again, until she came to a red wire, which she flexed from top to bottom, until she found a break in it.

Jumping up, she put her ear to her door to listen out for Fat Al and Frank, but the flat was silent. They must have already left for the Squawking Parrot, their favourite pub, she thought.

Der rummaged around in the base of the desk again, pulled out a soldering iron and plugged it in. Moments later she had expertly replaced the wire with another from a bunch of electrical spares in her desk drawer. She screwed the radio back together, put the batteries in and it burst into life. The local radio station blurted out a mixture of current popular music. She switched it off and delicately placed it in a carrier bag. She moved onto the next item, dismantled it and again expertly repaired the electronics.

Peering at an old clock sitting on her desk, she decided she had time to do one more. So next she picked up what looked like a toddler's toy. It was a large white cube with different shaped and coloured buttons on it, designed to make sounds and say the shape's name when a toddler pushed the button.

Der tried it, but the unit would not power up. She searched for a way to open it, but there were no visible screws, or clips. So she did what any budding fixer would do; looked for a join in the casing and carefully prised the casing open. The case hinged open with a smooth movement, revealing an extremely complex set of components unlike Der had ever seen before.

She was not in the slightest bit deterred though and found the intricacy of the minute circuits inside exciting. She set about trying to find the issue and before long found what appeared to be a built-in battery unit. When she went to touch it, a tiny static blue spark crackled, arcing across to it.

The battery glowed very faintly orange momentarily, before fading again. Der excitedly jumped up and rummaged around in her desk for various different batteries and brought them over to the toy.

As she held up an AA battery next to it to compare, there was a sudden tiny arc and then the toy battery glowed orange. It lasted for a few moments longer than her static had, but soon faded back to a dull metallic colour. Der did a double take; she had never worked on an electrical item that charged through proximity. But she had recently read about conductive phone charging in her favourite corner of the school library.

She took each of her batteries and brought them close to the toy, and each time the strange battery unit glowed momentarily and then faded. Next, she tried with the case placed over to see if it was designed to charge through the case, but the white casing stopped the conductive properties of the battery. She concluded that the case had to be off, and the power source had to be mere millimetres from the toy's battery in order for it to charge. Her eyes wandered over to the household socket in her room.

Der knew the very important rule of electronic tinkering, which was that mains electric can be really dangerous. In fact, it can kill you if you misuse it. She knew not to plug dismantled things into it, and to always respect it. But she reasoned with herself that she would not need to plug anything into it, just hold the battery part of the toy millimetres from it, and maybe, just maybe it might charge.

Der stood up and rushed over to the socket in her room. She knelt in front of it, her hand shaking with excitement, as she held the battery part of the circuit board millimetres from the socket.

***

It was a slow night at the Dirgefield power station and George, the operations manager, was just tucking into his eighth cup of tea for the evening.

'Did you see the game yesterday, Tony?' he said, while slurping his hot tea.

'Yeah, what a match! Can't believe they scored that last goal with only seconds to go,' Tony said with excitement.

Suddenly a whole array of red and orange lights

flashed on both their panels, accompanied by the soothing tune of screeching alarms!

George jumped in his chair mid-sip, spilling the contents of his cup all over his face and shirt, while Tony, who was just tucking into a jam doughnut, clenched the doughnut in shock sending the complete jammy goodness spurting out into George's eye!

What followed can only be described as 'pandemonium' as George and Tony jumped up to try to work out why the power station had been thrown into emergency protocol. As they gazed at the various panels, they squinted at the load readout. The dial's needle had shot up into the 'max load' zone and was still rising.

'Hey, we have to do something, or the station will...' George began to shout above the chaos, but his sentence trailed off into silence as the whole station including their lights went pitch black. A couple of phone torches flashed on, illuminating two very concerned faces.

'I'll phone the head engineer, Jerry, in the power station over in the next county, to see if he can help.'

Several phone calls later, and George turned to Tony. 'They are all down. Apparently from tip to toe of the country. Every power station has been overloaded.'

'What? All of them?' Tony replied, the magnitude overwhelming him. But just then, the station rumbled back into life and the lights all flickered back on. The dials on the readout all looked normal and none of the alarms were sounding. Tony and a rather sweaty, jammy, and tea-stained George staggered back to their seats and began to try to work.

CHAPTER TWO

Der had pulled the toy away from the wall moments after the electricity had gone out. She rushed to the window to see a scene she had never ever witnessed before.

The horizon, that usually twinkled like a starry night with household lights, was pitch black. Just as she began to become gripped by the thought that she had singlehandedly destroyed the national grid, and possibly wiped out the technology of the modern world as we know it, the lights all flickered back on. Slowly and tentatively, she brought the toy, which was still in her hand, up level with her face.

The battery glowed a soft tone of green and shimmered. She gulped and then sat back down to reassemble the case. After carefully closing the case around the circuit boards, she pushed some of the buttons. The various shapes lit up as she did so, but there was no sound. She dismantled the case again and painstakingly looked over the various parts and intricate circuit boards, until she noticed a series of micro switches on one of the boards.

On inspection with a magnifying glass, she noticed that two of the five switches were set to the '0' position. Carefully using a pair of tweezers, she flipped up one of the switches, replaced the case and pushed the triangle button. A voice said, 'Triangle,' and a giant smile swept across Der's face.

'Yes!' she whispered, as she punched the air. Deciding to test that the other buttons worked she pushed a square, a circle and then a hexagon. As her finger pushed the hexagon, there was an enormous flash of vivid bright blue light.

Der's room slowly faded into blackness like a dimmer switch had been used on all of the light. She felt herself moving and then had a churning, sickening feeling in the depths of her stomach.

Then suddenly she was travelling along a void, surrounded by what looked like streams of coloured light, each one moving at different speeds. Some raged, like frantic fast-moving lanes of highways and others trickled, ambling along, barely moving. Some even moved in the opposite direction.

Suddenly from one of the streams a humanlike figure flashed into view like an exploding firework. Der could momentarily make out a man wearing a metallic suit, like a space traveller from a far-off distant land. Just as she tried to study the image, it fizzed and disappeared.

Then, in another stream, another flickered into sight – this time it was a young girl, dressed in rags. In just a moment she became a lady, then an old bent-over woman walking with a stick, until she too fizzled out of being.

More and more images began to explode into sight, increasing in intensity: each one moving at different speeds, as quickly or slowly as the stream they had emerged from.

They were all dressed in different clothing, from different times. It was like watching a thousand movies all at once and all at different playback speeds. Some were caught on fast forward and others rewind, and some appeared to be paused for an eternity, barely moving a frame. As she picked up speed, tumbling ever faster, more and more images of people and creatures ignited into sight till like a finale of fireworks the people flashed so quickly she could not make them out and it all simply became a white light. Far off in the centre a coloured stream flickered, which she seemed to be falling towards.

The sensation of tumbling became more intense. The toddler's cube toy that Der had been holding felt hot to the touch one minute, but now in the dazzling white light her hand no longer registered its heat.

Suddenly her finger felt something wrap around it, metallic and hot. She studied her finger in the blaze of light. And there, wrapped around it was a simple ring with four shapes: a triangle, a square, a circle and a hexagon.

Der's mind began to run wild at the thought of the surreal shapeshifting, dimensional device she had awoken! But just as she began to process it all, the falling stopped. She felt something cold and hard beneath her. She squinted, but it was pitch black and deadly silent.

As panic began to grip her, sunlight broke the horizon, stretching and piercing into the black, silky world. She was lying on a metallic pavement overlooking a series of strange shops. People began arriving. But there was something wrong. Something really wrong.

The people were walking backwards towards the shops, then disappearing into them. A street cleaner, surrounded by bags of rubbish, was carefully taking the rubbish out of the sacks and placing each piece on the street and road.

A window cleaner was washing a clean shop window, but as he washed it, the murky water he used left the window dirty and not clean.

The shops opened and customers began to arrive, but they all arrived backwards, complete with large bags of shopping, and moments after entering they came back out again empty-handed.

She could hear people speaking in the street too, but the words echoed in a harrowing way, it was no language that Der had ever heard before and it was painful to her ears.

Panic flooded her as she began to forget even how she had arrived there. In a hazy memory she remembered the ring, and frantically she touched the triangle, the square, the circle and the hexagon on the ring.

There was a flash of vivid blue light and the people and place faded into blackness. The churning, gagging sensation came again, and she hurtled back through the void and past the great firework display. The white light faded, and she opened her eyes to find herself lying on the rough floorboards in her room, the kids' toy in her hand.

'Ah, I slept,' she said rubbing her eyes. 'What a dream.' She turned and looked at the old toy and felt determined to finish repairing it before she went to bed. She glanced at the clock on her desk, and it read 10:59.

'Now where was I?' she muttered, trying to remember. 'Ah yes, just about to test it.' She pushed the circle and sure enough the toy said, 'Circle.' Then she pushed the star; the voice said, 'Star.' Then the square; the voice said, 'Square.'

And as her finger pressed the hexagon, there was an enormous flash of vivid bright blue light once again. Der's room slowly faded into blackness. She felt herself moving and the same sickening feeling right in the depths of her stomach, but not as badly as she had the first time.

Suddenly she was travelling back through the void, the streams of coloured light surrounding her again, all moving at different speeds.

'Oh, it wasn't a dream,' she muttered.

Then the flashes of people ignited again – there were

a few she recognised from before but most were new. And again, in the crescendo of white light she saw in the centre the flicker of a coloured stream she seemed to be heading towards, but it was a different colour than before.

The cube toy was hot to the touch again and she felt something wrap around her wrist. It was a metal bracelet. It wasn't gold, or silver; in fact, as she strained to see through the brightness, she could make out that it looked like a child's bracelet, made of a cheap alloy and with four small glass shapes crudely set into it.

The shapes Der recognised: a circle, a star, a square and a hexagon. Der's mind began to run wild wondering what the device really was and why it looked like a toy! But just as she began to process this, the falling stopped and Der fell onto something soft and warm.

CHAPTER THREE

The white light faded away and Der found herself lying on her side staring up at a rich blue sky, the warm sun finding its way amiably through the canopy of a vast forest.

She squinted and lay there as her stomach settled. Slowly she scrabbled to her feet and looked around. Spectacular giant trees stretched up into the sky and between the trees was a thick untouched carpet of lush green moss, as far as the eye could see. A gentle breeze brushed through the forest, whispering as it went.

Der slowly turned in a circle, squinting at her new surroundings. The smell was musty like an autumn day after it has rained. She sat back down for a moment to let her stomach settle, a little dazed and confused.

'Where am I? And how did I get here? Maybe I am simply dreaming,' she muttered to herself.

But bathing in the warm sunshine and listening to the gentle sway and knocking of branches in the wind, she felt strangely at ease and relaxed.

She closed her eyes and listened. First, she heard the tapping of branches and creaking of wood, then as she listened more intently, she heard majestic birdsong floating through the forest, from place to place and bird to bird. Some of the sounds were simple like that of crows and others complex melodies that shifted and changed in time.

She had never been to a forest before, she was filled with complete awe at the splendour of the smells, sights and sounds. Startled, Der opened her eyes to see movement, as a large black and white striped bird landed close by. She stayed statue-still, observing it with curiosity as it began to walk around, rooting in a patch of soil close to a silver birch tree. Suddenly it began to peck at something, using its beak almost like a shovel to dig. Moments later its head emerged from the earth with a brightly coloured item in its beak. As soon as it had a firm grip of it the bird flew off in a rush, as if carrying off treasure.

Der walked over to where the bird was digging and rummaged through the dirt but could not find anything. She decided to walk in the direction that the bird had flown.

The moss was soft and springy under foot and her eyes flitted from tree to tree. Some were bulbous great trees with small pools of water in the notch of their branches, creating tiny micro ecosystems that housed water skaters and other insects that in turn were food for frogs and other animals.

Others were tall proud trees that pointed to the sky with spindly fingers. She meandered in and out of them trying to walk in one direction. As she was beginning to wonder if the bird had truly come that way, she caught a flash of black and white just a little way ahead.

She stealthily approached, rounding a final tree before she came upon a great ring of brightly coloured items. Sitting proudly in the middle was the odd black and white bird.

Der very slowly knelt down next to the coloured objects, half expecting the bird to scarper in fright, but it sat completely at ease with her.

It eyed her oddly, then did a funny little dance flapping its wings and turning in circles, before finally lowering its head and repeatedly tapping a crude wooden bowl-like object.

It reminded Der of buskers on the streets of her town. The bird kept tapping its beak on the wooden bowl. She reached down and picked up one of the brightly coloured objects. It was a strong yellow colour and rustled. She turned it over to see a shiny silver layer on the back. She brushed the mud off it and there in very faded ink was the letter 'Q'.

She placed it down carefully where it came from and picked up the next. It was bright red and round. She turned it over and scooped out the mud from its hollow underside. A wide smile swept across her face as she realised what it once was.

Yes, it was very faded and extremely worn, but it was a plastic bottle cap. The entire ring of objects were old bits of plastic that the bird had mysteriously dug up and arranged, almost like a salesperson – or should I say sales-bird?

Der stood to leave and the bird began to look flustered. First it did another frantic dance, bobbing and turning in circles almost like a dog chasing its tail. Then as Der took another step, the bird gave a guttural screech.

As she turned away, the odd creature leapt into the air, frantically flapped its wings, and flew towards her. Its sharp beak hit Der on the arm, just missing the old bracelet she was wearing, and she let out a small scream.

Looking around, Der could see that the angry bird was coming back for another strike. She fled, running as fast as she could. She ran and ran, till she could no longer hear the squawks of the bird. Eventually she slumped down behind a large oak tree to catch her breath.

Der clutched her arm. It stung. Wiping it on her trousers, she saw that the bird's sharp beak had left quite a deep cut and it was gushing with blood. With the fright and adrenalin she had not felt the pain, but she must have been bleeding for a while.

She looked down to see that her raggedy, patched jeans had blood on them too, from the gaping cut. She tore a strip off her shirt and tightly wrapped it around the cut just above her wrist. She glanced at the old bracelet trying to remember where it had come from, but it seemed of no importance, and her memory was hazy and broken. Her hand felt numb and the cut ached.

She sat still trying to calm herself when she saw something strangely familiar. Just a little way in front of her was a small dog. It resembled a mixture of a poodle and numerous other dogs. It looked like a stray, uncared for, its fur was like that of a wild animal, but still its size and features were unmistakably that of a poodle.

Wondering whether there might be someone walking the dog nearby, that she could ask for help, Der called out, 'Hello, is this your dog?'

The dog ran closer towards her, and she put out her good hand in order to let it sniff and to stroke it, but as it grew nearer, it snarled and bared it teeth. Der drew back, horrified by its wild and savage nature.

Then she caught sight of another dog, this time much bigger also coming her way, and suddenly there was a whole pack of them. All different mixtures of breeds but all wild, unkempt and coming towards her with only one thing in mind.

Turning to run, Der fled as fast as she could, her heart pounding, branches lashing at her as she crashed through the wild undergrowth.

They were gaining on her, and she could smell their hot festering meat breath. Just then she spotted an extraordinarily gnarly tree, with branches that twisted and curled close to the ground.

With a sudden surge of determination to survive, she leapt up, grabbed one of the low-lying branches and scrambled up to the higher branches.

Finding one that she could perch in, she squinted

down to see the pack of feral dogs barking and jumping up at the base of the tree. Snarling and gnashing their teeth, they jostled with each other trying to get onto one of the lower branches.

Der's hands were trembling with fear. She was a tough girl, putting up with bullies on a daily basis, but she had never been chased by wild animals before.

There was no reasoning or talking to them. They were simply hungry predators. And she was food to them, no different than a deer, or other prey. Petrified she sat still, her eyes streaming with tears and shivering uncontrollably.

The dogs looked like they were going to stay there in a frenzy, barking, growling and jumping up forever. And they probably would have done too, if it wasn't for that strange sound that echoed through the trees.

It was like some sort of call, but not in any language that Der knew. Then the call turned to cries and screams. The dogs one by one pricked up their ears. It sounded like someone or something was hurt, and the dogs thought so too.

All of a sudden, one of the larger dogs howled and sped off in the direction of the cries, and the rest sped off too, in hot pursuit of the first. There was a great sound of barks, snarls, cries and finally silence.

Der scrambled up into the top of the tree and finding a cluster of branches that acted like a natural hammock, she slumped into them. From there she could see what looked like the edge of the forest and somewhere beyond. Exhausted and terrified, she slipped into a feverous sleep cradled by the boughs of the tree.

Der woke abruptly. It was night-time, and the forest was pitch black. A shiver ran down her spine as the eerie sounds played tricks with her imagination. Then she realised what it was that had woken her.

Far off in the distance, beyond the edges of the forest, she could make out lights flickering and flashing, darting around, almost as if in mid-air over a sea-like landscape.

She gazed up at the night sky and saw a spectacular field of diamonds sparkling. And as she turned her head to look at the sky in the opposite direction, she spotted two moons. One looked very similar to the one she had often gazed upon at home, but the other was much smaller, yet bathed in a brilliant glow, as if made up of millions of lights.

She stared intently at it, trying to make sense of it and her day, and as her wild imagination sailed, she slowly and surely drifted to sleep once more.

The warm waters of the mid-morning sun flooded over the canopy as Der awoke, feeling groggy and tired. Her body ached from lying in that tree all night, but the heat of the sun was soothing and warmed her aching body.

Tentatively she edged her way down the tree to the lower branches to get a good look around and make sure the coast was clear, nervously dropping off the last branch onto the floor.

Still gripping onto the branch with both arms in case

the dogs appeared, she scanned the woodland as far as she could see in every direction. With no obvious sign of danger, Der decided to creep through the forest and get as far away from there as possible.

She tried to remember all of the events of the day before, in the hope that she might remember a detail that could help her. But the memory of everything before the forest was hazy, like looking across a misty moor.

She felt ambivalence, both excited to be in a strange and beautiful place, but also afraid. She wasn't sure whether to search for a way out or to explore deeper. Eventually her curiosity and excitement got the better of her. But as you know, curiosity can kill the cat. But so can the dog!

As she was creeping like a soft-pawed puma through the forest, she heard a familiar, yet unsettling sound. It was the same sound that she had heard the day before: a sort of chattering, but in a language that was completely unknown to her. Der concluded that language was usually a sign of intelligence and therefore, whoever or whatever it was, they might be able to help her.

She shifted her course through the dense woodland, to follow the voices. Swiftly, she moved closer, and with every step, the chattering became louder.

The canopy also began to thin out a little, and with it, the bright relentless sun streamed in. Der squinted for a while, half dazzled by the sun after having been in the dimly lit dense undergrowth for so long.

As Der's eyes began to adjust, she could make out a large bulbous tree standing on its own. Just then the speaking grew louder.

Der struggled to scramble towards it, as the floor was a criss-cross of large gnarly roots. As she made her way towards the trunk of the tree a little way off, she realised that the roots were becoming larger and higher as she walked, and strangely the voices were also becoming more frantic, almost like the crescendo in a piece of classical music.

The roots seemed to also be quite slippery; unlike the dry usual roots of the forest, they were oozing a slimy liquid. As Der looked around, she realised that the liquid not only covered the roots but had formed deep pools between the them.

'Stay where you are. Don't move a sinew!' a soft voice whispered.

The voice took Der by surprise, startling her so much that she almost fell off the slimy root and into the pool in front of her. She slowly turned her head to see a very tall figure standing quite close.

The man had long, fluttering grey hair, warm blue eyes and a wrinkled face, not with age but with smile lines, and skin that was the texture of sandpaper. His outstretched hand was covered in calluses and small scratches. His eyebrows were big, bushy and grey, and his ears disproportionately large to his face. He was thin; not wiry, but lean, like someone that spends their life walking and working on the land. He was wearing a crudely sewn waistcoat and loose-legged trousers made from a natural rough weave fabric, almost like sacking.

The two things that struck Der the most though, were not the roughness of the man's clothing or skin, but his kind and gentle smile. Well, that and the fact that this man was about nine-foot tall.

Some might say he was a giant, but he was hardly tall enough to be classed as such. But, at the same time he was taller than all other adults that Der had ever met, at least as far as she could remember. He was either a very tall man, or a very tiny giant!

Der gazed back at his kind eyes and instantly felt calm and trusting. She reached out her hand and he grabbed it, helping her back to the edge of the roots that she had come from.

CHAPTER FOUR

Only once Der was safely away from the roots did the tall man kneel down and speak to her, though his accent sounded strange. 'You are lucky, girl,' he said with a smile. 'You were almost as dead as a dingo!'

'What is that place?' asked Der, trying not to panic. The man took a deep breath and furrowed his eyebrows as he tried to think of the words to explain in a language that he seldom used.

'It is a kind of tree, a singing tree. Lost people and animals follow the singing and then fall in the soup!'

'Soup?' Der questioned.

The tall man pointed to one of the large pools and said, 'Yes, soup. It eats you.'

'The liquid dissolves people and animals?' Der said with confusion.

'Yes, and you were almost soup too.'

Der furrowed her brow. 'But trees don't sing and they don't eat people.'

The man smiled grimly. 'This one does. It is home to chatter-birds. The tree dissolves animals and produces small, sweet fruit that the birds feed on, so the birds lure people to the tree. A kind of friendship. But very dangerous for you. You come with me; I will take you to my village. It is safe there. You must be hungry from being lost in the desert.'

'I am very hungry,' said Der as she followed the tall man. 'But I haven't been in the desert.'

After a few minutes of walking silently he stopped and looked down at Der. Then he reached out his hand in a gentlemanly manner and said, 'I am Golderwin.'

'I am Der,' she answered, 'which is short for Derwin.' And Der took his hand and shook it. It felt strange for her; she had never shaken someone's hand before. Sure, she had seen teachers and adults doing it sometimes, but most of the people in her forgotten life greeted her by a push, or a punch, and that was if she was lucky. And here was a great tall man, stooping down respectfully to shake *her* hand.

Golderwin continued shaking her hand for far too long, muttering politely, 'How don't you do?'

Der smiled and said, 'You can stop now, and isn't it 'how *do* you do'?' The man looked down, embarrassed, and then stared at Der's eyes in confusion.

'Your eyes are different', he murmured to himself. 'You are definitely one of those desert people, but your eyes are strangely different.'

'I've never been to a desert in my life. What is strange about my eyes?' Der asked in surprise.

'Hmmm, well, your people all have milky eyes from the lack of light they get; you are the first I have ever met that has clear vivid eyes, just like my people,' he explained.

'You say "those desert people", so what are your people called?' Der enquired.

'We are called the Virdarians, but most of your people just call us the Foresters.'

'And what about the desert people, do they have other names?' Der asked

'They mostly call themselves the Wastelanders, but our people's name for them is the Aridians.

Just then he took a deep sniff, and at the same time his vast ears wiggled and twitched. A soft melody filled the air, he stood still, listening to every note and tone, almost like a great composer listening to an orchestra.

Finally he turned back to Der. 'I will reply to the message,' he said. Before Der could enquire what he meant, a low rumbling came from Golderwin. The tone and volume grew, until he let out a great booming tune. His melody undulated, and danced on the breeze, almost like that of a songbird. For such a large, wild-looking man, his voice was unbelievably beautiful. Then, almost as quickly as he had started, he fell silent.

'What was that song for?' asked Der.

Golderwin grinned. 'In the forest it is difficult to speak to each other, but a song carries on the wind. Many years ago, my people started singing to communicate, just like the birds. Over time, singing was favoured over speaking, and now we simply just sing.'

Der's eyes widened with surprise as she tried to imagine what it would be like to sing all the time instead of speaking. Her mind began to fill with questions.

'Wow, Golderwin, that's an amazing way to communicate. Where do you live? Can I meet your friends and family?'

Golderwin's smile suddenly turned to a look of concern. He abruptly knelt down beside Der and spoke in a low and serious tone. 'Derwin, you can come to my village, but I am really sorry, you mustn't be seen by my friends and family. Though they tolerate the desert people, they wouldn't welcome one of *your* kind in *their* village. I could get into great trouble by bringing you there, but I can't leave you lost. Not in the forest.'

For the first time in Der's life, she felt what it was to be cared for. It was a strange feeling, and quite alien to her. Trying to distract herself, she asked Golderwin, 'So what did your people say in their song just now? It sounded like something really complicated and meaningful.'

Golderwin's smile shifted to a small laugh. 'No, it was my wife, she was reminding me to check on the saplings.'

Der smiled and said, 'I guess songs make even the mundane sound beautiful!'

'We have a lot to do, before we visit my village', said Golderwin. 'Follow me and only tread where I tread. The forest can be dangerous unless you know your way. Oh, and try to keep up!'

And with that, he twizzled around and began to bound through the forest, his legs springing like on a trampoline. Der followed him, her feet falling into the indents on the springy moss left by his large feet.

Shades of green flashed in her peripheral vision as she tried to keep up with her new friend. Der was grateful that the Virdarian knew his way around, and for the first time since she had arrived in the strange place, she was able to move without getting tangled, scratched, or snagged in the undergrowth.

The jog was hard going though, in the warm humidity of the forest. As beads of sweat began to trickle down Der's face, Golderwin stopped abruptly. He raised one of his eyebrows and held up his hand to signal Der to also stop. Then he tiptoed very gently into a small clearing where there appeared to be lots of young trees growing.

Der crept tentatively into the clearing, being careful to only tread where Golderwin had. He knelt down at each young plant, inspecting the leaves and springy young stems

Der listened as Golderwin spoke about each tree sapling and sang their Virdarian names.

'The names sound so beautiful in your language,' Der said. 'Do you think you could teach me some Virdarian?'

'It is very different from your people's language, Derwin, but I will try. I will use some Virdarian words as we work and speak and you can try to sing them.

When the two of them had checked each of the trees, Golderwin knelt down at an empty patch and from a small fabric bag that Der had not noticed before, he took out a handful of tiny seeds.

'Would you like to plant some?' Golderwin asked. Der had never been in a forest before, let alone grown anything. The closest she had ever come to it was a culture of mould that she had grown in a cup when she was a small child. She had felt especially lonely at the time, living in Frank's flat, and she thought that she could sprout a friend. Needless to say, Frank had thrown it all away and banned her from using cups, forever! So, when Golderwin had offered her this chance, she was overwhelmed with excitement.

'Will it grow if I plant it? How do I do it?' she blurted out in enthusiasm. Golderwin reached into his bag, rummaged for a moment, and pulled out a small wooden trowel, which he handed to Der.

It may have been small for Golderwin, but for Der it was a awkwardly large. Yet she found that by using two hands, she was able to dig a small hole. The soft soil was spongy and rich in colour, and when the trowel dug the soil, a pleasant moist woodland fragrance wafted around Der's nostrils.

'OK. Now you can gently put the seed into the hole and cover it with the soil,' he whispered. Der carefully followed his instructions, finishing the job with a good dose of tapping down the soil. 'OK we can come back tomorrow to check them,' Golderwin said.

'Why do you plant them?' Der asked.

'Well, it is our job to take care of this forest,' said Golderwin, with a hint of pride and honour. 'It is the last of its kind, so my people tend to it. We plant new trees when old ones die, we clean it, we make sure it is healthy and we protect it.'

'But what do you protect it from?' Der asked.

'Well, from the hungry desert and the even more hungry people!' Golderwin said.

'What hungry people?' Der asked curiously.

Golderwin broke into an odd chuckle, expecting her to chuckle too. But she stood staring at him, with a confused look all over her face. When Golderwin realised, his eyebrows furrowed so much that they almost met in the middle.

'Your people, Derwin, the desert people. They come to the forest to take everything they can carry, with their beastly devices that use the blue fire. Some come to trade, which we tolerate, but others just take. You must know what I am talking about, desert girl?'

Der was bewildered and didn't know what to say. She tried to explain. 'I'm not from the desert. I don't remember quite how I got here, it seems hazy, but I'm not from your world!'

Golderwin laughed a deep roaring laugh then spoke. 'Girl, maybe you are too young, or have lost your mind, but you are of desert family. Look,' he said as he pulled out a wooden bowl, filled it with water and placed it on the ground like a mirror.

'Look at your short figure, your pale skin and your tiny ears. I am typical in looks for my people the Virdarians. Look at how different I look to you!' His tone was kind but firm.

Der glanced down at her reflection then up at his bright glimmering eyes, his bronze tanned skin, his taller than normal build, his long muscular legs and his oversized ears. He did look different.

'Centuries of living in the forest, working outside, bounding and singing has formed my people and distinguished them from yours. We are all human, both your people and mine, but our lifestyles, heritage and attitude towards nature have set us apart.

'But don't worry, I am not like most of my people. I recognise that your people and mine share more similarities than differences – we are all people after all! Others, sadly, only see the differences and this is why you must be careful in my village *not to be seen*!'

Der opened her mouth to protest and to explain that she came from somewhere else, but every time she came close to remembering, the memory slipped away. It was like trying to hold onto a wet fish or keep sand from sliding between her fingers. She decided to just go with it, at least until she could remember how she got there and then tell Golderwin something concrete!

'Next we must go to visit a fantastic little creature,' Golderwin continued. 'It is right up your road!'

Just then Der thought of a question that was bugging her. 'If your people only sing now, and don't speak anymore, how do you know how to speak my language?'

Golderwin's eyes twinkled. 'Ah, to answer that, I would have to show you. But not now and not yet. Later! Now this peculiar creature, you will like this!'

Just as abruptly as before he twizzled round and began to bound off into the woods. Der was overwhelmed by everything she had seen and heard over the last day but had no time to ponder or process it, not if she wanted to keep up with her new friend. So she took a deep breath and loped off after him.

Springing on the soft moss like a long-pile carpet, she went. Flashes of blues, greens, reds and golds whizzed by in her peripheral vision, almost like a rich dreamworld at the edge of her perception. But she never once looked back. She kept her eyes fixed on Golderwin's flapping waistcoat, like a young cub following its parent.

She hurried on, weaving in and out of the trees to track him as he meandered through the forest like a needle through a sheet of fabric. After a while he slowed and ground to a halt.

Stepping gently through the undergrowth, he came to a tiny clearing, which Der immediately recognised. Filled with panic, she edged her way behind Golderwin and cowered. She rubbed the wound that was still weeping a little blood above her wrist, remembering that savage and irritable black and white bird. She glanced at the bracelet momentarily, before she peered around Golderwin's leg to see what was happening and watched as he rummaged, his hand in his sack, feeling around for something.

'Aha,' he said with triumph as he pulled out a piece of soft-looking bread. On the ground was the same bird that Der had met earlier, surrounded by its items and bowl. It splayed out its tail plumage, almost like an oriental fan, then it spun round and round doing a little dance, almost like a dog chasing its tail. Golderwin broke off a piece of the soft bread and placed it in the wooden bowl, then he inspected each of the items in turn until he came to the little faded red bottle cap. He reached down and tapped it.

The bird squawked in reply as he picked up the bottle-cap and placed it in his bag. The bird went back to its dance, this time even more frantically, till Golderwin put more bread into its bowl and chose another item, this time a square object that had a triangle and the word 'play' faintly written on it.

Adding the last piece of bread, he selected what looked like a small broken torch. Golderwin tapped the torch and the bird replied with a confirmative squawk. The Virdarian put the torch into his bag and closed the flap. As if on cue, the bird stopped dancing and bowed its tiny head.

Golderwin wheeled around and began to stride off. Der looked at the bird, which she could swear narrowed its eyes and glared at her. Terrified that the bird would attack her again, she dashed off after Golderwin, peeking back every so often to make sure the bird was not following.

They jogged through the forest for what felt far, far too long. In fact, Der was about to protest and demand that they stopped, when Golderwin slowed to a halt at a small glade. 'This is our herb garden,' he said. 'Don't touch anything here. Some can season your meat, others can make you kick the pail!'

Der tilted her head to one side. 'Kick the pail? What do you mean?'

Golderwin smiled. 'You know, kicked the pail! It is a phrase meaning to die.'

'Ah, you mean, kick the bucket! I see.'

Golderwin hung his head slightly for a moment and said, 'Ah, sorry, Der, I might mix up some of the phrases from your language, I don't speak it that often.'

'It's OK, Golderwin, speaking another language is difficult. You're doing just fine!'

Golderwin led her tentatively into the glade and Der watched as he darted around to different plants, picking ripe vegetables, and fruit reciting their Virdarian names in song for her to try. While Der tried to copy his song, she smelt a sweet and delicious smell as it wafted past her in the breeze. As she wandered towards the smell it became stronger, and her eyes began to flutter with tiredness. She stumbled to her knees as her whole body ached and became numb.

Golderwin was speaking about the various plants he was harvesting with his back turned to her. His voice became echoey and distant till it was a rumble and then just a distant murmur on the wind.

Suddenly her eyes snapped open and she could see a rather concerned Golderwin inches from her, wafting a pungent flower under her nose. The rumble of a voice came back, then the rumble merged into words.

'Derwin, Derwin, are you alright? I told you not to touch anything.' She was back in the middle of the glade, away from the beautiful smelling plant.

'Yes, I am OK now,' Der said groggily.

'You got too close to the dreamy plant. It is a distant relative of the soup tree and also is carnivorous. Its smell attracts animals and as they wander too close, just inches from the plant, the spores are so concentrated that they send you into a delicious and comfortable sleep. And the more you sleep, the more you breathe in the spores, blissfully unaware that the plant is beginning to feed from your nutrients.'

Der gave a shiver at the thought of being devoured alive whilst in a blissful sleep. 'So how did you save me?' Der asked, her heart still thumping in her chest from such a scare.

The Virdarian opened his hand to show a brown finely-ground powder. 'This is from the wake plant and is a relative of the plants that people used to farm for coffee a long time ago.'

Der reached into his large bowl-like hand and took a pinch. She held it to her nose and took a long and deep breath in. The brown dust had a rich smell, aromatic and invigorating. Sure enough, there was a hint of toasted coffee to it.

'Take some of the dust and put it in your mouth,' Golderwin said with a grin. And with that he took a pinch and jammed his finger into his mouth rubbing it on the inside. Der looked away, disgusted!

'And now you!' Golderwin said with a wink.

'I'm not putting my fingers in my mouth!' Der said as she folded her arms and stood bolt-straight in defiance.

'Well, if you want to harvest some of the dreamy dust with me and catch our supper, you will need to use wake-wake dust. Well, that is unless you like eternal dreams!'

Der reached forward and pinched more wake-wake dust and self-consciously rubbed it all over the inside of her mouth.

Golderwin led her to the dreamy plant and the two knelt down in front of it. Der was amazed to see that the dust had no effect on her now that she had the wake-wake dust in her mouth. She intently watched him twist off several powder pods from the plant and empty the yellow acrid dust into a leather sealed bottle with a cork-like stopper.

She followed him to the middle of the glade where there was a fallen tree that doubled up as a seat. Golderwin rummaged into his seemingly bottomless bag and pulled out a bunch of thin, papery leaves. He measured out a tiny amount of the dust into each leaf and twisted each one into a tiny parcel, no bigger than a fingernail. Then he stood up and said, 'Let's catch tonight's supper.'

The two of them crept through the forest, using the moss to cushion and silence their movements. A little way in and Golderwin crouched down, still as a statue, only his hand moving silently to a Y-shaped catapult that was hanging from his belt. He reached into a leather pouch that he had filled with the tiny pea-sized parcels of sleepy dust and loaded one into the catapult.

The catapult was formed from a branch and some sort of black rubbery material with a small leather cup that the sleepy dust peas sat in. He carefully took aim, held his breath and released.

There was a loud 'twang' and a puff of yellow dust a way off into the forest, as the leaf pouches burst. There was a blur of movement nearby and Der watched as some sort of small creature jumped a few paces into the forest, before slowing, gently lying down and dozing off into a relaxed sleep.

'There,' said Golderwin with satisfaction. 'Much better than bows and arrows and the horrid weapons that your people use. Come and have a look.'

They walked over through a patch of long grass and knelt at the sleeping animal. Der smiled as she realised she recognised it.

'It's a rabbit!' Der exclaimed, running her fingers through its fur. 'But why is it green?'

'All of the rabbits here are green,' said Golderwin. 'What other colour would they be?'

'Well, grey or brown!' Der replied, not knowing how

she knew that.

'I don't know that I have ever seen one those colours,' replied Golderwin thoughtfully. 'Not adults anyway. They *are* born grey, but their fur soon turns green. It is the result of an algae that lives in their fur. It is another friendship! The algae helps to camouflage the rabbit and in turn the rabbit lets the algae live in its fur. If you live and work in a forest for long enough, you will come to feel and understand the strange relationships of every living thing.

'This mighty forest is a whole community of living things, from the tiniest fungi that help the trees communicate, all the way up to the snoozing honey-bears. Each has its role and maintains a delicate balance; the balance that we tree-folk help to protect and keep.' Der listened intently as she gazed around the forest in awe.

'But how do you know that eating the rabbit won't upset the balance, if it's such a delicate one?' Der asked.

'That is a good question, Der, and one that your people never ask. You seem very different to all the other desert people. Well, when you live and rely on the forest to be your very home, you soon become aware of the waxing and waning of animals at the different times of the year. We only take what we need and when we do, we always put something back. From our childhood we experience and learn these rules. Our elders show the children how to track animals, to count and keep an eye on their numbers; how to live and work in harmony with the cycles and times of the forest; and to listen to the voices of the forest.'

Der looked at Golderwin in disbelief. 'What do you mean voices? Trees don't speak and neither do animals!'

Golderwin's face shifted into a warm smile. 'No and yes is my answer, Derwin. Of course, trees don't speak, well not in the way that you and I are speaking at the moment. But if you are truly observant and use all of your senses, you can read the forest. Let me show you!' he said as he stood up and walked over to one of the trees.

'When you look at this tree, what do you see, Derwin?'

There was an awkward silence as Der was not sure what she could say. 'A… tree!' she said mischievously.

'Look at the colour of the leaves; they are a little pale compared with the other trees,' he said. Der gazed up at the old and gnarly tree. Far up in the branches above she scanned the colour and noticed the difference.

'Yes, I see that,' she said.

'Now smell the bark,' he said. 'What do you smell?'

Der smelled it. 'It smells of peanuts.'

'Yes, Derwin, that is right. The smell is an excretion created by the tree when it is attacked by insects. The tree has been attacked by a small beetle larva. They usually live in small enough numbers not to damage a whole tree. But this cycle, there was a surge in rabbits, which the larvae often use as transport, hitching a ride in their fur. The rabbits are overpopulating the forest this year, because spring came early, and the winter was very mild.'

Der was astounded to hear about these relationships and asked, 'What else was affected?'

The Virdarian smiled. 'Everything. And I could spend years showing you how to read the forest and its inhabitants!' he replied. Just then a flock of bright green sparrow-like birds flew overhead, chirping as they went.

Golderwin glanced up. 'We have to go,' he said urgently. 'There is a danger coming. Strong… er, what do your people call it? Wind, yes that is right and maybe even rain,' he said repeating the same words in Virdarian song. 'Those birds nest on the very rim of the forest and are very sensitive to the changes in the desert. When they fly this close to the heart of the forest, it means… er… batten down the hatches, as your people would say.'

Der was about to ask a question but realised that Golderwin had already scooped up the sleeping rabbit, reeled around and loped off.

'Never mind,' she muttered, as she bounded off after him.

CHAPTER FIVE

They jogged through the forest rapidly, as the sky grew darker with every passing minute, until they came to an area deep in the centre, surrounded by truly ancient trees that towered up into the gloom.

'We are here!' Golderwin announced.

'Where?' Der managed to say, between big gulps of air.

'My village,' he replied with a tone of pride.

'Er, I don't see anything,' Der gasped. 'Just these trees; where is your village?'

'Look up!' said Golderwin, gesturing with a grin. Der looked up to see the most magnificent sight: high up in the strong branches of the trees were beautifully built tree-houses, gently nestling in the crevices of great branches.

Each one was different in shape, hugging its tree. Long elegant rooves curved over the yellowy wooden structures. They had small windows cut into the sides, with a latticework of woven leaves instead of glass. Between each house, rope walkways criss-crossed the whole village.

As the wind began to strengthen, the trees very gently swayed and so did the houses, firmly nestled in their branches like babies in their parent's arms. 'This way!' Golderwin gestured urgently. 'My house is on the other side of the village.'

They dashed between the great trunks to the other side of the village, where there stood a truly, ancient and gigantic tree. Among the topmost branches was a small house, but what struck Der as odd was that leaf-surfaced windows had also been cut into the tree itself. Der opened her mouth to ask a whole new load of questions, only to be silenced and frantically beckoned by Golderwin.

'Quick, this way, Derwin; danger is coming close and we need to get into the safety of the tree.'

He led her around to a beautifully made door, made out of hand-cut planks of wood which had been lovingly secured together and hung in a frame cut into the tree trunk. Golderwin opened the door and beckoned Der inside. Once inside he secured the door with a wooden beam.

'Unlike the other trees in the village, this one is hollow,' said Golderwin with glee. 'It still stands strong, but I have made some of our house inside it.'

Der peered around to see a vertical tunnel running up to a plank floor. The inside of the trunk was a smooth texture, a deep rich brown. A spiral staircase ran from the ground up to the floor above and the dim evening light streamed through the yellowy-green leaf windowpanes. Der could just make out a hatch on the ground near her feet.

'Where does that lead?' she asked.

'Ah, that is very special, but unfortunately that will have to wait for another day. Let me get you settled into a small room on the next floor up. The room was once my son's, but we don't use it anymore. Well not since…'

Golderwin's eyes looked away and his voice trailed off. Der noticed that the corners of the strong Virdarian's eyes were filled with tears.

'What happened to your son?' Der asked in a soft and concerned voice.

Golderwin turned his head back to Der. 'My son Arberwin is alive, I know it!' he said, his eyes welling up. 'But… but… maybe I will tell you another time. For now, let's get you settled in and safe.'

He took a step forward and stooped to her level with a look of concern. 'I will tell my wife you are here; she won't be happy about a desert person being in her home, but she too would not leave you in the forest alone. Don't wander around the house and stay out of her way; she is far less tolerant of your kind than me.'

The spiral stairs creaked and groaned as Golderwin climbed them and Der followed, taking large steps to clear the uncomfortably high stairs. Round and round they went, the light waxing and waning as they passed the tiny leafy windows.

Golderwin turned the handle of a dust-coated door

and it grated open. A large window was set in the centre of a semi-circular room, filling the room with a soft green light.

'I am sorry everything is so dusty in here,' said Golderwin. 'We don't come here anymore. I will bring you some rabbit later. We are not great at cooking meat, because we don't often eat it; only when there is an abundance and it helps the forest.'

He slipped away before Der could reply. It appeared that every moment in that room churned his stomach and racked his heart. Der looked around at the soft curves of the inside of the tree, which made up the walls. The room was sparsely furnished apart from a hand-woven rug and a large bed mat made of the same kind of fabric as Golderwin's waistcoat and stuffed with soft material. A few garments made out of natural fibres were hanging on pegs and there was a large pair of leather slippers which Der put her feet into, giggling as she realised that she could put both feet in one slipper.

Der sat on the bed roll and listened to the wind howling outside. She watched dreamily as the green windowpanes cast fluttering flecks of light onto the walls like dancing butterflies. The tree gently swayed in the wind, letting out tiny creaks.

She closed her eyes and tried to visualise where she had come from, or any detail that she could pluck from her memory about her life before the forest. But it remained cloudy and distant. The harder she tried, the mistier it became. It was useless; she could remember almost nothing.

It was strange, because she remembered feelings and words, but not enough to recall the whole picture. The tree's swaying increased and Der felt a little alarmed. Before it had felt like being gently rocked, but now it was like being buffeted.

Just then there was a soft knock at the dusty old door. 'Hello,' Der whispered. The door swung open and in walked Golderwin with a tray of food, which he placed down next to her. 'Enjoy your meal, Derwin. I hope you sleep well too.'

Der looked at Golderwin in panic as the wind lashed at the outside of the tree, causing it to sway alarmingly with a creaking groan.

'The wind is really strong tonight; will we be safe in this tree?' Der asked with a little fear in her voice.

'No problem, Der,' Golderwin answered. 'This tree is very strong and has withstood many a day of what your people call wind. Or we call…' He paused and then hummed a short sequence of melodic notes. 'But I must admit that the *wind* does seem to be becoming more frequent and damaging recently; it used to be a very rare thing even a few years ago. Now it even sometimes comes with…'

He shifted to a melodic song for a moment, expressing a word he only knew in Virdarian, and then noticing the fear still in Der's eyes, he continued in a reassuring voice. 'But you have no reason to fear. This tree has been around for almost a thousand years. It has seen so many things, both happy and sad, including its fair share of wind and wars.'

He took one final glance around at his son's room, wrestling with sadness and regret, and slipped out of the door before Der could speak any more.

When the door clicked shut, Der was left alone with the creaking tree and lashing wind. She glanced around at the inside of the room and muttered, 'A thousand years. Wow.'

Comforted in that knowledge, she turned her attention to her dinner. Tucking into the simple steamed food, she was suddenly overwhelmed by the flavour and purity of it. There were no seasonings, yet she could almost smell the fresh forest air, and taste the rain and soil in each bite.

Der ate heartily, leaving the rabbit till last. She had no idea what to expect, as she wasn't sure if she had eaten rabbit before and had the feeling that meat was a scarcity in her life before the forest. She tentatively took a tiny piece of the meat and popped it in her mouth. It was succulent and delicious, so Der devoured it rather quickly, mopping up the juice on the hard wood plate with the hearty chunk of bread. She placed the plate and wooden spoon beside the door and settled back onto the bed. As the evening light played across the ancient wooden walls, she slowly drifted off to sleep.

Der opened her eyes, to find herself for the second morning in a row in a strangely unfamiliar place. Slowly she glanced around at her surroundings, her mind blank for a second or two, till the memories came flooding back.

She sat up, wondering what had woken her. There it was again. A lone bird cry. Not complex or rhythmic, but strangely unsettling. An echoing lone chirp, that seemed to almost be calling out, 'Is anyone awake?' And between each call there was an empty silence as it waited, perhaps considering whether it might be the last bird, in the last forest in the world.

Then without warning, as the first warm golden fingers of the sun reached down into the forest, a second bird answered. Then another and another. Then other birds, with a rich diversity of melodies began to sing.

The dawn chorus in the Last Forest was not diluted, like in a city, but a loud and gigantic celebration of a new day. What the birds were communicating, Der could only wonder, but she had never heard anything like it before. And then suddenly, almost as quickly as it had started, it subsided.

Der got up and stretched her aching limbs. Chasing after Golderwin the day before had left her muscles sore; she had never run quite so much in her life. Just then there was a soft knock at the door and Golderwin entered. He carried a small plate with some soft bread on it and a hot liquid.

'Brought you some breakfast, Derwin,' he said with a smile. As Der tucked into her breakfast, Golderwin said, 'We have a big day before us, Derwin. But first we have to sneak out of the village before most of my people wake up and go out to tend to the forest.'

As soon as Der had finished eating, they descended the spiral stairs to the forest floor and cautiously slipped away into the cover of the trees and set off.

The first stop was at the young saplings that they had tended and the seeds they had planted the day before. Der-noticed that the seeds had already popped up.

'See, even a desert pirate can grow trees,' said Golderwin. 'Though I bet you must be the first. They usually cut them down.'

Der stroked the soft yellow leaves of one of the saplings, wondering if the tree might grow to be an ancient one like Golderwin's tree and what animals it might home.

After checking each of the saplings, Golderwin led Der out of the clearing and further into the forest.

Just then Virdarian song rang out into the wood, carrying on the wind, like the leaves of the very trees that surrounded them. Replies rang out to and fro. And all the time Golderwin stood still, his oversized ears like antennae listening. When the last of the replies faded into the forest sounds, he turned and looked at Der.

'It seems they have called a village meeting,' he said. 'We were due to be tending to the forest all day, but we have been called back, which means there must be something really wrong.'

'Come on,' Der said. 'We will be late for that meeting!' And at once Golderwin was left in a cloud of mossy dust. But he soon caught her up and was striding along next to her. Turning his head as they ran, he tried to speak between puffs.

'What do you mean *we* will be late for the meeting, Derwin?' he asked.

'You know, the meeting! If it is urgent, maybe I can help,' she said.

'Let me get one thing straight, Derwin,' Golderwin replied sternly. 'There will be no *we* at that meeting. If my people catch you in the village, they will be very angry, tie you up and take you to the desert. And that's if you are lucky. Some might want to feed you to the forest!'

He screeched to a halt in front of her, causing her to almost collide with him. She found herself looking into two large and stern eyes. The soft and gentle tone had gone for a moment and Golderwin spoke in a firm voice.

'Derwin, this is not negotiable. You must not be seen, or even thought about by my people. Your people and mine have a very old and brutal history, and the hatred runs deep. We have had many wars and lost many of the village family to them. Even I have lost…' His voice trailed off into a whimper.

'Your son?' Der enquired softly.

'Yes,' he continued with a pained voice. 'Arberwin was taken by a group of desert pirates near the forest edge years ago. I know he is still alive, but could be anywhere now. Derwin, do you understand the risks and difficulty I took by rescuing you? I too dislike many of your people, but I could not leave you to fend for yourself in the forest. If it had been one of the other villagers, they would have just left you. So, don't get seen by anyone at any cost.'

The run back to the village was sombre and silent, with neither of them wanting to speak. Der snuck into the tree when the arriving Virdarians were not looking and waited in her room.

The bedroom she sat in now took on a different light, an empty reminder of the son that had been taken. It didn't seem such a comfortable place to be any more, especially if it was indeed *her* people that had taken him.

She pondered the words *her people*. Was she really one of them? She began to wonder if she *had* been and that maybe she had lost her memory.

A Virdarian song from the centre of the village echoed through the thick tree-walls and Der realised that the meeting had started. She listened curiously as the melodies bounced backwards and forwards in an odd musical conversation. The to and fro started gently, but soon became the song equivalent of an argument. The tone and volume changed, becoming gravelly and loud; a rumble of sound that caused the very forest to tremble, rising to a sudden crescendo.

At last the song subsided into a babbling stream of tunes before dissipating entirely, and the forest sounds became prominent again. Moments later Golderwin tapped on the door.

'Follow me! I have something to show you!'

CHAPTER SIX

They descended the winding stairs within the great trunk, and at the bottom Golderwin reached towards the floor, scrabbled around and took hold of a metal ring. He pulled it hard and lifted an ancient rickety trapdoor, then stepped down into the hole and disappeared, before reappearing and beckoning for Der to follow.

She slowly followed him down into the gloom, at first stumbling on the creaking stairs, till her eyes adjusted to the dim, but not pitch-black place. Eventually they reached a solid floor below the twisting and turning stairs.

Der found herself in a gigantic cave beneath the tree, yet strangely it was not completely dark. An illumination from the ceiling cast a soft yellow glow over everything, enough to make out most of the strange environment.

'This cavern is older even than the tree,' Golderwin murmured, his hands firmly planted on his hips, and sounding like a tour guide or historian. 'It has been used by my family for generations, for countless purposes. My great-grandfather used this place as a secret bunker during the great desert pirate war. He used it to plot the attack that saved my people and paused the feud. I say paused, because though now we tolerate each other, we still feud. My mother used it as a place to map out every inch of the forest and keep our most important records.'

Der looked around at the vast collection of objects. She pointed to a wall at the opposite end with a set of handmade wooden drawers that stretched from floor to ceiling. 'What's that?' she asked.

'Ah, that is not mine,' he replied. 'It belongs to the whole village, but I take care of it as it needs darkness and safety. It is our village's collection of seeds; we harvest them every year and use them to plant trees and vegetation mostly in places where your people have cut and taken everything.'

Der looked away, feeling somehow responsible for the damage the desert people had done. She peered around the vast cavern in awe. 'And you; what do you use this place for?'

'Ah, let me show you.' He led her down a narrow aisle with boxes and makeshift tables on either side brimming with odd objects. Der wanted to stop and take a closer look, as familiar shapes flashed by in her peripheral vision, when eventually she found herself standing at an age-old desk.

The desk was different in colour and style to the other things in the village. Golderwin sat behind it in what was once a small and rickety red leather chair. It looked too small to be made for a tall Virdarian. He took out the small items that he had bartered for with the bird and placed them on the table, rustling through his dusty and dishevelled books. Der could not hold her curiosity any longer, she had to have a good explore.

She started looking at the objects, each one had a note attached to it, almost like that of labels in a museum. She picked up an object and gently inspected it.

It glinted in the yellow light and somewhere deep in the caverns of her mind memories stirred. Not solidified, concrete images of days in her life, but words and understanding. She gently rolled it around in her fingers. It had a long handle, split into three prongs that were twisted and bent.

'Beautiful isn't it!' Golderwin whispered beside her, with the air of a historian's authority. 'This was used by our people's ancestors to scratch their backs when they were bitten by itchy insects.'

'No, it wasn't,' Der blurted out. 'It was used as a way to eat, a little like you use wooden spoons. Look, the prongs are bent, but if we straighten them you can use it to stab food and put it in your mouth.'

There was a moment of silence, while Golderwin reeled at the fact that his historical hypothesis had been unpicked by a desert girl. Der stood still in confusion; somehow she knew the object and its function and was absolutely resolute about the fact that she knew. She picked up another object, long and cylindrical, made of a faded ornate plastic with a sharp tip at one end.

'That was used by our people to write with,' Golderwin said with certainty.

‘Yes, it was dipped into ink and used to write, but later they used ball pens.’ Again, the words that came out astounded Der. She could not work out where and when she had gained this knowledge, but it was absolutely clear in her mind.

‘Wow, you are quite the historian, Derwin,’ he replied. ‘I know that your people have a liking for ancient tech and objects, but you really know your stuff. How about this?’ He gestured to an object the size of a plate, a slightly mean glint in his eye, as if he wanted to really put her to the test.

Der picked it up, and turned it over in her hands. It was perfectly round and resembled a plate; it had geometric holes, and on the underside’s centre was a curious symbol. Her instinct formed words that seemed to bypass her conscious knowledge. ‘This looks like a plate, but it isn’t. It’s a car wheel hubcap!’

Golderwin looked perplexed and studied the object with a furrowed brow. ‘It is a what?’

Der explained that it was used to cover the metal wheels on cars, a form of transport, and make them look pretty. Again, she had no clue where this encyclopaedia of information was coming from.

Golderwin turned, walked off and rustled around on a table covered in very old and delicate books that were just *that bit* too small for his Virdarian hands. He carried a small book over, cupping it in both hands like it was a fragile egg.

‘I have traded these books over my lifetime, mostly

with some of the gentler desert pirate groups. They are some of the rarest items to be found; the fabric they are made of seems to degrade.'

'Paper,' Der said, glancing down at the pages. 'It isn't a fabric, but I guess they are delicate.'

Golderwin turned to a small picture of a vintage car.

'Yes, look there on the wheels,' Der said. 'They are metal, but later they were made of plastic.'

They wandered over to the pile of books on the table. 'These are how I learnt your language,' Golderwin explained. 'I remember my first book, when I was a tiny child. My father and I were out at the edge of the forest, which was a lot further away in those days.

'I was watching him trade with a group of desert pirates called the Foragers, when I spotted the book on the pirates' boat. I asked my father if he could get it for me and very reluctantly the pirate leader agreed to swap it for two loaves of bread. I cherished the book, even though I could not read a word. The pictures inspired me to find out more about history and that is when I started to collect ancient objects from the forest.

'My father thought it was a little odd but said at least I was not harming anyone. And my mother let me use a small place down here to catalogue my first archaeological finds. I spent almost all my childhood here in this very room, excited about my latest finds, dreaming of what each object was. Words and text slowly seeped into my mind and little by little I picked up language.

‘I would also accompany my father to the edge, where he would trade and tend to the vegetables that we use to make the bread. I went at every opportunity, just to listen to the strange language that your people spoke. My father never understood it; he would just use gestures and smiles to clumsily communicate. Little by little I began to pick it up, till one day as a young adult I helped my father explain a trade he wanted to make to the desert pirate group, and soon after that, it became my job to tend to the forest borderlands and lead the trading parties.

‘No one else could speak to the pirates and traders, and most were afraid, because the edge is patrolled by not only traders, but aggressive desert pirates too. Some came to steal, or to damage the forest, some to attack my people.’ He trailed off with a sigh, glancing down at Der sadly.

‘Derwin, I have a few things to do here for a while. You can look around and explore my museum while I am busy.’

And Der did just that. The objects spoke to her; there were all sorts of things, from fragments of packaging to parts of engines and household items. But most of all there were broken pieces of electronics.

As she browsed the objects, she found an old lamp. Then she got carried away on an idea that made no sense to her, yet intuitively she felt a pull towards it. Soon she was dismantling the broken muddy parts of an old calculator, removing the solar panel, and wiring it up to the lamp's LEDs. She could not understand why she knew how to do that, but her hands just did it.

'Ha ha!' she exclaimed, as she turned on the circuit she had managed to create out of old museum objects. The LED bulb flickered and then lighted dimly. 'Look, Golderwin, look at this,' she said, jumping up and down with glee.

Golderwin peered up from his preparations, and rather than joy, a look of utter shock came over his great face. He rushed over, snatched the circuit, threw it to the floor and stamped up and down on it heavily. Der, so shocked by his actions, burst into tears, breaking Golderwin's moment of rage.

Panting after his outburst, he turned to a rather soggy tearful Der. 'Derwin, I am so sorry. You must not make or repair electronics here. That is one of the great rifts between your people and mine. Technology is strictly forbidden in our forest. Look around, Derwin, all this stuff was once used and part of our people's civilisation so many years ago. Not much is known about that time, only what your people salvage from far away ancient places and I find here. An even greater mystery is what changed the world to make it as it is now, but what we do know is that it was technology.

'It is not right to use electricity, or other tech; it damages nature and makes our people lazy and greedy. We tend to the forest and will not permit anything that could damage it. We must keep the harmony and the way. Your people, though, they use that blue fire, electricity, to aid their existence in the Wastelands. It is this that divides our people, and… you and I.

'I am sorry, Derwin, but you cannot stay here; you do not belong. You should be with *your* people.'

The Virdarian's words cut deeply into her heart and yet seemed to make sense to her too. But not wanting to give up so easily, defiantly she said, 'I don't want to go and live in the Wastelands, I like being in the forest. I can learn the Virdarian ways.'

'No, Derwin, you can't live here,' he replied. 'It is only a matter of time before you are seen.'

'I could live in the forest, away from the village, and you could visit me every day,' she said with determination. 'I could help you take care of this place.'

'No, Derwin,' he said firmly. 'The forest is shrinking at an alarming rate; it is not a safe place for a desert girl to live.'

'And the Wastelands are a safe place?' Der scoffed.

'Derwin, our bread supply was destroyed in the wind last night. The winds are becoming more frequent and according to my people the forest is being destroyed at an alarming rate – a rate never seen before. Soon my people will live in the Wastelands too and the Last Forest will die and be forgotten, marked only by the pages of these fragile books.' Tears trickled down Golderwin's face as he said those last words.

'What is destroying the forest?' Der enquired with concern.

'The winds can damage the trees and bring desert,' he

explained. 'But most of all, it is the groups of rogue pirates that cut down the trees and take everything in the night. Without a way to stop them from poaching and deforesting, we have no home and no chance.'

Der wept at the thought of the Last Forest becoming a wasteland because of her people. 'Surely you can do something to stop them?'

'My people have all agreed that the only way to stop them is to fight, despite my efforts to suggest more peaceful ways,' Golderwin said. 'I have bought us all some time, but I can see a great rage growing in my people's hearts, one that will lead to blood being shed again. I can't tell if it will be only a series of battles, or an all-out war, but their hatred for your people is now wide awake and their fierce need to protect what is left means violent times are surely ahead. I must find a group of pirates or traders that will give you safe passage to one of the Wasteland towns as far away from here as possible and if I can, find someone there to give you a home.'

Der was surprised to hear that she would be leaving the forest almost as quickly as she had arrived.

'I am gathering some of my most valued electrical finds to trade for your passage and set you up in safety,' he said.

His compassion for Der, despite *her* people having taken his son Arberwin, made her weep and she hugged him, looking up into his kind eyes. 'Will I ever see you again?'

Golderwin's face twisted into a look of fear. 'Derwin, I hope not, because next time we meet we might be enemies. I implore you to get as far away from here as possible.'

The Virdarian stood up abruptly with a look of determination and the stern face of a general before a mission. 'We must leave first thing tomorrow morning and travel the whole day in order to get to the forest-edge by early evening. There we will camp for a few nights and await your people. Derwin, I need you to have an early night. The journey will be long and dangerous, but out there on the edge will be the most dangerous of all. Pirates of all kinds patrol the desert by night.'

Der nodded sadly and began to climb the twisting stairs for an early night, leaving Golderwin to pack their provisions and plan their trip.

CHAPTER SEVEN

As Der lay on the soft bed roll, her mind was in turmoil. She felt like a boat in the rapids, barely able to take stock of things before she found herself washed away into another part of the river. She lay tossing and turning, unable to rest, her heart filled with sadness, anger and confusion.

If only she could remember her life before the forest. Maybe she had parents out there in the desert towns. She cast her mind back to that first day in the forest, but it was even more hazy than the last time she had tried to remember.

It was early in the morning, with the first fingers of sunrise and those lone birds crying out, when Der finally fell into an exhausted sleep. And only a few hours later, there was a soft knock at the door.

Der awoke bleary-eyed, momentarily content until the memories of the night before crashed down the door and lumbered into her mind. She realised that it was the day she was to leave and she remembered why. The soft knock came again at the door and Der mustered a weak, 'Enter.'

It was Golderwin, wearing a long cape and his usual shoulder bag, this time it was even more full to the brim.

'It is time,' he said softly. Der got up and solemnly followed him down the spiral staircase for the last time, out into the cool crisp morning air as they sped off into the cover of the forest.

After a few moments of striding in silence, Golderwin stopped, and turned to Der. 'It is especially important to stay very close to me. Don't touch anything we pass and take this.'

He handed Der a wooden pot with a cork in the top. She opened it and was surprised to see thousands of sleepy dust peas, the little leaf packages that she had watched him make out of the dreaming dust. Then he handed her another small pot, this time with a wider mouth and cork. He gestured to his mouth and she realised that it was wake-wake dust. She pulled the small cork out and rubbed a little in her mouth. Before she could ask any more questions he had started off again.

Der worked hard to keep up with him, but unlike the short bursts of the days before, Golderwin was leading her on a long journey. But the thought of being left behind, getting lost, or eaten, was enough to make her keep running.

After two hours on the move she began to falter. The sweat was in her eyes stinging them, her heart was thumping, and her whole body was weary and exhausted. She had nothing more to give, and though her mind was filled with the fears of the forest, her body said no.

She stumbled and swayed until her legs gave way completely and she tumbled to the soft mossy floor, lying in a crumpled heap. She could hear the leaves whispering above and feel the gentle breeze cooling her cheeks.

'It is OK, Derwin,' a gentle voice whispered. Soon she was being bumped and jolted around and lifted through the air, coming to rest on Golderwin's shoulders. The last thing she remembered was the gentle bumping of Golderwin carrying her as he strode on through the forest.

Der awoke by the warmth of a glowing fire. Golderwin was stirring a small pot of food he had set on it. Wisps of steam eddied and twisted from the pot with a delicious aroma that wafted in Der's direction. Her body ached all over.

'I see you are awake, Derwin!' Golderwin whispered with a warm smile. Der tried to stand but fell back in exhaustion.

'Easy now, Derwin, rest. You exhausted yourself trying to keep up with me. You are far smaller and not used to forest bounding. I had to carry you the rest of the way.'

Frustrated and determined, she stretched, stood and walked over a little closer to the fire where Golderwin was cooking and sat cross-legged. He passed her some soup and she ate.

'Where are we anyway?' she said, looking around for some clue to their location. 'I must have been out for hours.' All she could make out was the trees around her glowing in the firelight and the dark haze of the forest beyond.

'We are on the fringes of the forest, Derwin,' Golderwin said, as he scooped up a great handful of dry soil and threw it on the tiny fire. Instantly the fire died down to a very soft glow and the darkness of the forest closed in around them like a great scarf.

'Look over there, Derwin, but stay quiet,' he murmured. They sat in silence staring out into the blackness, listening to the eerie night-time sounds of the forest. After a while, Der saw a flicker of light dancing far off on the horizon, quickly followed by another, then another. They were all flying in different directions, some bright and shimmering, others faint and barely glowing at all.

'Desert pirates and traders, Derwin,' Golderwin whispered, 'racing through the desert off to some distant place. Trading, plundering, exploring, stealing. Some are kind people just trying to make their way in life, trying to make enough food to feed their families or clans. Others are ruthless slavers or pillagers, stripping trees or attacking their own kind. Every night they come out all over the desert. It is the only time it is cool enough and the wind consistent enough for them to sail.'

'Look, there's one coming towards the forest,' Der said in excitement.

'Derwin, I want you to stay hidden if they come this way,' said Golderwin, deep concern in his eyes. 'They might be your people, but some are ruthless killers and slavers.'

Der agreed and watched silently. The light came closer, and as it did it became brighter, till they saw it stop on the edge of the forest and heard a great rowdy sound of laughing and shouting, wailing and crying.

All of a sudden, the trees far off at the edge began to rustle aggressively, then in an ear-splitting crack that seemed to silence the very heart of the forest, a tall tree thumped down to the ground. The ground around them rumbled. There were cracks of whips and whimpers, and another tree began to shake.

Golderwin stood up in silence and strode off, signalling Der to carefully follow. They double-backed around to a better place to see what was happening and finding an old half-rotten wind-fallen tree to hide behind, they kept watch.

A huge man stood close by with his arms folded, dressed in strange leather armour. He was tall and lean, his eyes milky white and his cheeks red, but his face was engulfed in a great brown beard which encircled most of his features. He wore an odd flat cap to one side and a long heavy coat. Hanging from his waist was a thick chunky belt housing an assortment of objects. Der could make out a long-curved sword that hung to one side.

'Faster, you bunch of maggots,' he bellowed. Instantly his six crew members lashed their whips at a small group of slaves consisting of men, women and even children.

Some were working hard to work two-person saws, with one person on either side of the log. Rocking backwards and forwards, the pairs worked in unison to cut the great felled tree down into smaller pieces. None dared to pause for a breath or even look up from their work, as they knew it would be met by lashes. They looked barely fed, unwashed and some had visible wounds.

All the time the flickering lights of the monster-like vessel that they arrived in, bathed the forest in a cruel red glow. The vessel was like nothing Der had ever seen – even if she could remember what she had seen. One giant mast stretched up into the air with a huge makeshift sail hanging from it, and a black flag emblazoned with white keys flew atop the mast. The ship seemed to be a mixture of old steel sheets and timber beams, with fabric stretched over some sections, as though it had been cobbled together from spare parts. And unlike a conventional ship, the hull was flat and sat on four wheels. The back of the ship had a giant loading bay that was dropped down to the sandy desert.

Once the slaves had finished cutting the tree into smaller pieces, the captain yelled out with a blood-curdling scream, 'Load it!' The crew lashed their whips in the air to punctuate the captain's order. Some of the slaves rushed over to a large winch as others wrestled the logs into place for the winch to pull them aboard the massive ship.

'She's almost full, Cap,' said one of the crew timidly.

'Alright, you scum,' the brown-bearded man bellowed. 'Let's sail this load back. Croge, Flina, and Sterg, stay back to hunt. Our food stores are getting low. See you on the second run. I just hope these slaves will make a few more cuts and runs.'

At that, two thin men and a rather burly lady pulled out bows and electric lamps that appeared to be home-made from foraged technology. The rest of the slaves and crew climbed up the ladders and ropes they had dropped from the ship. After pulling up the back loading flap, the slaves were shackled to large metal loops protruding from the deck, where most of them passed out from exhaustion.

The crew scurried about like a well-oiled team. A young man shot up the mast like a monkey and sat at the top, in what looked like a seat that had been lashed to the top of the mast. There he strapped himself, adjusting the seat's position with a series of levers.

'All clear, Cap!' he shouted in a high-pitched voice.

'Hoist the sail and release the brake!' the captain screamed. Immediately there was a grinding sound as the makeshift brake system was released and the sail billowed out in the wind. The ship trundled away through the desert, picking up speed as it went.

One of the remaining pirates passed close to their hiding place, looking disgruntled and bashing the side of the lamp she was carrying, which kept turning on by itself. 'Stupid thing,' she grumbled. 'I swear I always get the worst stuff, just because I am a girl!'

Her companion let out a nervous laugh. 'No, no, Flina, you know that no one would want to upset you! Here, take mine. Right, let's hunt.'

The three of them walked deeper into the woods, their lamps off and their bows at the ready. After some time, Der saw the light flickering on in the distance and heard the twang of a bow, as the crew shot arrows at the startled animals that were caught in the light.

Der turned to Golderwin to say that they surely could not be her people, when she realised that he had gone.

Looking towards the distant light, she saw a shadow among the trees and heard a twang. Moments later, Golderwin was returning with two sleeping desert pirates slung over his shoulders. After going back for the third, he tied them up by the felled trees and left a hastily-scribbled note jammed into one of their leather jerkins.

You are not welcome here. Let this be a friendly warning. If your people continue to take our trees and destroy our forest, we will be at war again. The Virdarians.

'Derwin, let's go,' he said solemnly. 'We have to get out of here before the rest come back.' Without another word, he threw her over his shoulders and was off.

They bounded for hours before emerging once again at the forest's edge and Der could make out a faint glow in the distance. Golderwin let out two booming notes of a forest song and she saw the small vessel change direction and head towards them, whistling as it came.

A much smaller vessel than the cumbersome logging ship, this was a sleek vehicle with a black sail and a curved bow that ended in a spiral of delicate carved wood. The vessel was mostly made of thin timber with refashioned fabric stretched over the whole hull and sides. The wheels were thin and spoked like the wheels of a bicycle and were set at an angle for speed. On top of the mast flew a flag bearing the insignia of skull and crossbones. A tall man stood boldly at the prow.

As the ship came closer, it looked like it would hit them head-on, yet at the last moment it did a ninety-degree turn sending a shower of sand over them. The sail dropped and a plank made from an old door was dropped down. The man at the prow strutted across the ship and down the ramp.

He was dressed in an elegant tricorn hat topped by a single feather. A dark, heavy coat flapped and swirled around behind him, over a smart waistcoat. From under his hat a long head of silver hair fluttered in the wind. He had a long, crooked nose and piercing stern eyes. A strange assortment of makeshift objects hung from his belt, some apparently made from wood but entwined with wires. Hanging from his ears like earrings were a string of foraged accessories which Der recognised as electrical diodes and she realised that the dusky grey pendant suspended on a necklace was a microchip.

Slowly and elegantly he walked towards them, while his two crew members stood firm at the entrance to the ramp, their eyes fixed on their captain. Both were thin and dressed in long heavy coats, but neither wore hats. Their hands curled around the hilts of curved scimitars.

The finely-dressed captain strolled up to the Virdarian, his unblinking gaze defying emotion. Der started to take a few steps backwards; the captain's gaze was so intense, it looked like he would cut both Golderwin and her down in a split second. Only at the very last moment did the captain outstretch his arms towards Golderwin with a smile.

'You old rascal you!' he exclaimed in a deep, gravelly voice. 'Why did you leave it so long? Heard the old call as I was passing!'

'Captain Silvaran, you old sea-dog, I have not seen you for many moons,' Golderwin boomed as they embraced. 'Where have you been?'

'Ah, I've just come back from the Far Wastelands and the glass mines. Got attacked by a couple of opportunist pirate gangs and delivered someone to the frontier beyond the Snakelands. You know, just the usual stuff,' he said in a modest tone, with just a hint of a smile at the very corners of his lips.

He reached into his pocket and took out a single glass lens that he had had fitted into a wooden surround. It hung on a string cord like a monocle. 'Picked this little gem up in the glass mines,' he exclaimed proudly. 'I can read again with this!'

They both laughed and then Golderwin looked concerned and lowered his voice. 'Who would dare attack the great Silvaran?'

Captain Silvaran let out a long laugh. 'You know, Golderwin, most people like to have a pop, some for the treasure they know I trade and carry, others for a chance to say they took down a legend! But most can't even keep up with the *Dawn Eagle*, and the others that can always get the point!' He cracked the joke with a dry tone, and an unchanging deadpan face.

'That reminds me, Golderwin, I have something you might like,' he said. He gave a low-pitched whistle and one of his crew members darted up the ramp, returning moments later with a fabric-wrapped bundle. Another appeared with a small table made from a rusty old radiator propped up on four makeshift legs.

Silvaran placed the bundle down and carefully unwrapped it to reveal a thin fragile magazine. Half of the front cover was torn and missing and mud and age had stained the rest of the exposed areas. He carefully opened it up to reveal faded articles about computers.

Golderwin looked excited, forgetting for a moment his gruff tone and speaking in a high-pitched explosive sound. 'Wow this is a rare one! Look at the detail preserved. Some of the articles are still readable. This one is about the first ever computer.'

Silvaran smiled. 'I knew you would like it. Are you interested? We can come up with a fair exchange for an old friend!'

Golderwin was just about to start bartering when he remembered Der standing behind him. 'Silvaran, I have a favour to ask you. It is really important and I am willing to pay you whatever it takes.' He stepped to one side to reveal the timid Der that was hiding behind him.

'This is Derwin,' he explained. 'I found her alone deep in the forest. I have protected her best I could, but she does not belong here. There is a war brewing again, old friend. The loggers are back and are cutting down vast areas of the forest. My people are angry and unless something can be done, we will end up at war with your people again. Derwin needs to be with her own kind; somewhere safe, far away from here.' He paused to gauge Silvaran's reaction.

Silvaran looked concerned when he heard mention of war, then he glanced at Der and his face shifted into compassion. Next he did something that you would not expect from a legendary pirate captain; he dropped down to one knee and extended his hand. 'Pleased to make your acquaintance, missy,' he said, a smile threatening to emerge from his stern face.

Der reached out and shook his hand. 'How don't you do!'

Silvaran glanced at Golderwin. 'See she's picking up your phrases!' he said with a chuckle.

Golderwin looked grave. 'I would like you to take her as far away from here as you can. Find her a family to live with, who will take care of her. She cannot remember who she is or where she is from. I have a little saved up,' he said, reaching into his bag and placing down several artefacts, each of which caused Silvaran's left eyebrow to raise higher in surprise.

'These are some of your most prized finds, Golderwin,' he said in a shrewd tone. 'Is this little girl really worth it?'

'Yes, she is,' he sighed. 'I don't know why, but I have a feeling she is important. And anyway, I can't leave her to get eaten by the forest or killed in the fighting between our people.'

Silvaran eyed the items carefully. 'Well, this is enough to get her to the Fringetown far from here, and pay a family to look after her till she is old enough to make her own way in the Wastelands. I have an old and very good friend there who I trust. We must leave soon though.'

Golderwin waved his hand at the objects, gesturing his agreement. 'So be it. Thank you, old friend. I know that you are a man of your word and if anyone can get her to safety, it is the great Captain Silvaran!'

Silvaran smiled and gave a short whistle to his crew. As they loaded the objects and the table onto the ship, he handed Golderwin the computer magazine bundle.

'Here you are, old friend. Take it!' Golderwin reached out and gently placed the item in his bag.

'What would you like for it?' he asked.

'Nothing, call it a gift from one friend to another.' And with that he gave Golderwin a hug, gestured to Der to board his ship and strutted back to the prow.

CHAPTER EIGHT

Onboard Silvaran's ship, Der felt timid and worried. The ship was small yet had an aftcastle, a lower deck with hammocks to sleep in and a small but very well secured treasure room. Everything other than the fabric and wood that made up the structure was refashioned from old familiar objects.

The wheels were made from bicycles, the mast from an old pole and the door handles were an assortment of radiator valves and taps. It was odd for Der seeing so many strangely familiar objects so out of context. The whole aftcastle was made of an upturned car bonnet with upright metal sheeting lashed around the edges to offer some defence if the ship were attacked.

'This is Slemp,' Silvaran said gesturing to one of his crew, a short and stocky man, with strange markings running down his muscular arms.

Slemp grinned at Der. 'Pleased to meet you, missy,' he said in a kind voice.

'And this is Bline,' Silvaran said gesturing to the other crew member a thin subdued man, dressed in simple brown garments who had scars all over him.

Bline nodded. 'Hello, missy,' he said.

A voice from an unseen crew member boomed out from way up in the mast. 'Cap, are we baby-sitting again?'

Feeling slightly indignant at being called a 'baby', Der stared up to the top of the mast. She could just make out the silhouette of a girl a few years older than her, perched on a makeshift platform.

She had long black hair with a white streak running down the middle and wore a jacket that looked as if it was taken straight from Silvaran's wardrobe. Around her waist was a thick black belt hung with an assortment of devices, including several strange telescopes and – to Der's surprise – a sharp curved sword. Over one eye was a strange collection of lenses that swivelled up and down.

As Der's eyes continued to explore the crew member in the crow's nest their eyes collided with a clash, and she looked away sharply. Despite her youth, the girl had a stern fire in her eyes.

'Pipe down, Arc, and play nice with our guest,' Silvaran called up, taking control of the situation much to Der's relief.

'Alright, Cap,' Arc replied, and with a sudden blur of motion she was at the bottom of the mast standing in front of Der and fixing her with a cold stare. Her face was stern and she had the stance of someone that was always ready to fight.

Der was afraid at first, but suddenly she found a

strange but familiar feeling dwelling up inside. She could not remember where or even when it was from, but an instinct of blatant and reckless determination took over. Like facing a bully at school, she knew she would probably be beaten, but would refuse to cower.

She met Arc's stare and the two became locked in a battle of determination. Her surroundings became hazy and Der could feel her heart pounding in her chest. Fear surged through her veins but she refused to give in. Neither blinked, neither moved, till suddenly Arc's hand was on Der's shoulder, a massive grin shattering her stone-cold face.

'Finally, someone with a bit of spice!' she said, as Der breathed at last. 'Nice one, girl.' Composing herself, Der timidly smiled too. 'What's your name and where are you from, girl?' Arc asked.

'I'm Der,' she replied. 'And I… I, well I don't remember where I'm from, but I've been staying with Golderwin in the forest.'

'I am Catrine,' the older girl replied. 'But my friends call me Arc. I'm second in command here and Silvaran's apprentice!'

Der took a small step back. 'Wow, that must be exciting learning from a legend like Captain Silvaran!'

'Aye it is, Der, but it's also very dangerous,' she answered.

'Will this journey be dangerous?' Der asked tentatively.

'Almost certainly! At least we can hope,' Arc said with

glint in her eye. 'But don't worry,' she said, detecting Der's fear. 'You're travelling with a legend and if you stick with me I'll keep an eye out for you!'

Suddenly a whistle went out as Captain Silvaran stood at the prow in the forecastle looking out over the desert dunes. The sleek black sail shot up the mast and instantly caught the strong wind. The ship whooshed away smoothly and before long the dunes were flashing by.

Suddenly Silvaran was standing by Der. 'What do you think of her?' he said in a gruff voice, gesturing to the ship without turning to look at her. The words hung in the air for a moment, while Der contemplated what to say to a legendary desert pirate about his ship.

'She really is fast, Captain Silvaran… sir!'

'Fast enough even to outrun the Fulgur!' Silvaran exclaimed proudly.

'The Fulgur? What is that? Another pirate or ship?' Der asked tentatively.

'Don't tell me you have never heard of the Fulgur,' Silvaran said in astonishment. 'Every desert traveller knows of it! Few may have seen it first-hand because it is so rare, but everyone old and young has heard the tales.'

'No, I haven't!' Der broke in. 'What is it?'

'Descriptions vary,' he continued. 'But I can tell you that the Fulgur is a gargantuan creature that roams the desert. It spits blue fire and smashes ships to pieces, eating everything, crew and all – well those that are not fast enough to outrun it!'

Der took a small step backwards in horror at the thought of such a beast. 'Is it out in the desert tonight?'

'Don't worry, missy. Though it *is* truly terrifying, it is rarer than water to see out here,' Silvaran said with slight unease in his voice.

'Have you ever seen it?' Der said her eyes fixed on the captain's.

Silvaran's eyes flickered in discomfort and he looked away for a moment into the hazy distant dunes. When his gaze returned he cleared his throat and continued hastily, 'Where were we, missy? Ah yes, mi ship! She is a real beaut isn't she?' he asked.

'Yes, sir. How long have you had her?' Der asked, curious about Silvaran's shift in topic.

'A long time! She was built to explore and transport treasures from horizon to horizon! And she has been me pride and joy since I were a lad, a long time ago now. I set out when I was not much older than Arc there. Born in the Edgeland slums, where work and life are hard, and the bread is even harder. I left onboard a pirate ship more than eight decades ago, as a ship-hand.

'I soon made a small fortune after getting lucky in the landfill mines. I saved for five long years, working under a grizzly and formidable captain. When I had enough saved, I had the *Dawn Eagle* built, and then made my own way!'

Der listened to Silvaran's story with great interest and asked questions as the night whittled away and the dunes sped by, though she didn't mention the terrifying Fulgur again.

'Slashers starboard-side on collision course!' Arc shouted in a gleeful tone. Silvaran spun round and taking out a homemade telescope set with old lenses he scanned the craft that was slowly approaching.

'Ha ha! You will have to try a lot harder than that. Amateurs!' he said with a smile and steely calm. He whistled a little tune and a call went up: 'V sails!' Arc was back up the mast faster than a bolt of lightning.

One of the crew pulled on a lever and an old antique motor churned into action. Two additional masts dropped down from the main mast on either side forming a large 'V'. Two more black sails billowed out and the ship lurched forward. The dunes flashed by so quickly now that they were a blur and Der felt queasy.

'Face the front, Der,' Silvaran said. 'It will help with the desert sickness!' The craft that was on course to intercept them was left in a cloud of sandy dust, forcing it to a halt. Before long they had lowered the additional 'V' sails and returned to normal speed. 'Don't worry, missy,' said Silvaran. 'That speed is enough to make even me queasy, if we hold it for too long.'

Silvaran looked up at the stars and the moon and appeared to calculate the time. 'We don't have a lot of time to get to Balldock before sun-up.'

Der focused on looking straight out over the bow, but it was no use; her stomach was churning and she just managed to get to the edge of the ship before she 'blew chunks'. After she had been sick, her stomach settled, and she was able to focus on looking forwards.

***

Under the steel light of the moon far from prying eyes and ears, two great ships had stopped and two figures stood facing each other, the moonlight glinting off their milky white eyes, their long menacing shadows stretching over the dusty desert floor.

Both were formidable in appearance, dressed in heavy coats to keep out the cruel desert wind. One was bearded, with a distinctive flat cap set to one side. The other was a woman, tall and broad-shouldered, her face pearl white with perfect slender lines and not a single blemish or scar. A collection of keys was jangling around her neck.

A scream came out from the vast ship behind her, and she spun her head round in a flash, her eyes ablaze. 'Silence that wretch!' she yelled out. 'Can't you see Dorlan and I are talking here?' At once the scream stopped and silence settled again on that dusty wasteland.

'Sorry about that, Dorlan, you were saying?' the tall lady continued, addressing her companion. Drawing his scarred and rugged fingers through his beard, he spoke grimly.

'Well, Satisa, I was logging early this evening. Left a few of me crew to do some hunting while I took the first load back, to find on my return me crew had been attacked by those barbaric Virdarians again! Left beaten and unconscious with a note threatening war!'

Satisa raised an eyebrow. 'War, you say? They are nothing but trouble those Virdarians. Refusing our people wood and food, while we struggle in the desert. It's about time they were put out of business for good!'

'Now that is an idea, Satisa. But how? There are so many of them and we can never find them in that forest, even if we could fight them all.'

Satisa paused to ponder the idea, her eyes filled with cunning and her mind at work like a train at full steam. 'Yes, how can we get rid of those dumb forest keepers… for good?' She didn't wait for an answer. 'A war! That is what we need.'

'A war you say, Satisa. But how will that help?'

Satisa smiled cruelly. 'Well, it would draw them out of that forest and mean that the other Wastelanders would do the fighting for us! Naturally, we would not get too involved and just take care of any Virdarians left afterwards.'

A look of excitement swept over Dorlan. 'Oh, I like that, Satisa. It would leave the forest open for us to take whatever we wanted, whenever we wanted. If only there was a way to give them all a helping hand, a little push!'

Satisa considered the idea. 'Yes, I like that, Dorlan! If we rile them up enough, cut enough of their precious forest that they feel threatened, they will become more and more aggressive with the other pirates that arrive at the forest. It will be only a matter of time before they kill a few too many pirates and the pirates kill a few too many of them. Only a matter of time before war becomes inevitable.'

Her eyes glinted as she continued in a cold voice. 'And if we force them into an all-out war, we could let them kill each other and then take that forest for our own. We could fortify it, move in and start charging anyone and everyone else left, for… well everything! We would control the water, the food and the wood.'

Dorlan smiled, glancing around to make sure they were still out of earshot. 'So let's up our game. We must enlist other ships, take more slaves and cut the forest *every night*, leaving nothing left.'

'Now you're talking, Dorlan. And whatever you can't carry home from the forest, burn. Let's make those Virdarians' blood boil.'

'So that settles it!' Dorlan roared. 'We shall slave and log every night, like there's no tomorrow. Take as much as possible. Then watch as the Virdarians and pirates kill each other and get very rich doing so. Sounds like a plan to me! There might be a couple of other captains that we could bring in too. But let's keep this tight! We don't want old Silvaran getting wind of it.'

The two captains roared with excitement, then turned and boarded their ships. The sails went up and the two ships went their separate ways, leaving wisps and clouds of dust.

CHAPTER NINE

The *Dawn Eagle* sailed on, deep into the early hours of the morning. Der's eyes were heavy and hazy when finally the call went up from the mast: 'Balldock ahead, Cap!' Der squinted but could not see a thing. 'Der, hold on tight; we're coming in fast,' Arc shouted down with a grin. 'You are going to love this bit!'

Just as the first few hints of orange appeared on the distant horizon, the sky fell away as the crew dropped the sails and the *Dawn Eagle* whizzed down a large sand tunnel, leaving the desert dunes behind and cruising on deep below the desert.

At first it was pitch black in the tunnel, with just the glow of the ship's lamps lighting the way. Then little by little a soft light could be seen ahead of them, till suddenly they emerged into what looked like a gigantic domed sports stadium.

Many centuries ago, it had been a magnificent structure at the centre of a bustling metropolis. Now it was completely submerged by the desert above and sand trickled in through cracks in its vaulted roof. It had been used as a ship dock for as long as anyone could remember.

Der gasped to see rows and rows of makeshift docking platforms, with all sizes and shapes of odd ships. People were milling around each of them, chatting, trading and arguing. The noise was immense. Lights were set up here and there, dotted all over the dock. The docking platforms followed the curve of the stadium, with rickety platforms leading to what had once been the various exits.

'Der, I want you to stay very close to us here,' said Silvaran beside her. 'This is no place for a young'un. This is the great Wasteland hub, Balldock. People come here from all over to resupply, to trade, to gamble, make deals and to rest. It is a kind of port. This is the only place in the Wastelands where ships cannot engage and crews cannot clash. But despite the truce here, there are still ruthless law breakers. After all, it is the desert's biggest melting pot!'

He whistled a long low pitched tune and the three crew members surrounded Der, keeping her at arm's length. Arc sidled up to Der. 'Don't worry; me and Scar here have your back!' she said while tapping the long, curved sword hanging from her waist. 'I won't let anyone hurt you.'

The crew walked with great swagger. After all, their captain was practically a legend. Der was amazed to see that the traders, slavers and other pirate groups, no matter how tough they looked, all moved aside to let Silvaran through. Nevertheless, Silvaran's hand remained firmly on his sword hilt at all times.

They made their way slowly to the nearest stadium exit, a task that took ages, despite people's polite standing aside. Apart from the sheer amount of people bustling around, there was also a great hum and buzz of speaking and there were odd smells too, grime and unwashed people, mixed with food. But the thing that Der noticed the most, was that everyone was very thin and pale, with milky white eyes.

The exit opened out into a series of wide tunnels which had been shored up by anything that was to hand; metal sheeting and ancient wooden beams. People sat at the edges of the tunnel, with odd objects laid out in front of them, selling things, or offering games and bets, deals or knowledge, all in the hope of making enough food to eat.

The tunnels were a blur of noises, smells and flickering half-broken lights. Eventually, they came to a sliding door made from an old tabletop. They ducked as they all entered the room it led to and closed the door behind them.

Inside was a small space dotted with makeshift tables. They were all different heights, some made from old crates, others from plastic sheeting, and around them were the old and tired seats from the stadium, which had been fixed in place to make them approximately the right height for the tables. They sat around one and Silvaran called out, 'Buzzers all round.'

The small thin waiter, who was scurrying frantically

between tables, hurried over at once, without making eye contact. 'Welcome, Captain. Is your credit good?'

Silvaran pulled out a handful of coloured glass fragments which caused the waiter's eyebrows to hit his hairline in surprise. 'Sorry, sir, yes, yes you can have anything that you would like!'

'What is there?' Der whispered to Silvaran. He turned his face sternly towards her and with a hint of a smile said, 'Buzzers, or buzzers!'

Moments later, five simple plates appeared on the table, a couple were pieces of slate and the other three slivers of old wood. In the centre of each one was a pile of crispy insect-like creatures. Strangely they smelt quite appetizing, though it was several minutes before Der found the courage to try one, and she waited to see her new companions ate them first. But when she did, she was pleasantly surprised. They were crispy and tasted like chicken.

'Sorry, Der, we don't have the variety of food you did in the forest,' Silvaran said in a very low whisper. 'Here in the tunnels and the desert wastelands, very few things grow. People farm insects, as they can tolerate the dark damp conditions and grow quickly. They are sustaining enough and make up our people's staple; that is, the ones who can afford food.'

Der felt suddenly humbled. She ate the rest of her buzzers with gusto, watching and mimicking Arc as she pulled the crunchy legs off first, then slowly chewed the bodies savouring the taste.

Silvaran turned to the flustered little waiter who was in a frenzy of serving, taking orders and running from table to table and said, 'Rock-wine all round.' Moments later, the man reappeared with five oddly shaped drinking vessels. One was an old wooden cup, carved from an ancient piece of timber, and the other four looked like they had been fashioned out of scrap metal.

Der stared at the odd liquid. Even against the tarnished metal she could see that it was not crystal-clear. It was very cloudy and had a gritty silt in the bottom. 'What is this, Arc?' she whispered.

'That's the finest water, Der,' she explained. 'Water is very hard to come by in the desert, but there are several natural underground springs. Rock-wine is the water that's taken directly from the spring source. It's the cleanest and best, but it costs far more. Most water comes from further down the stream and is much less clear than this.'

Der gazed at the brown cloudy liquid and realised how much easier life was in the forest, with its abundance of food and its crystal-clear springs. She watched as Arc drank heartily despite the grit and sediment and so she did the same.

Silvaran suddenly stood up, swaggered over to the waiter and dropped a single nugget of rich blue glass into his hand. 'But sir, that is too much,' the waiter said timidly, without making eye contact.

'Make sure your family eats well this week, Tweeb,' he said.

The waiter, bowed his head several times in gratitude. 'Thank you, sir, you are always generous, sir. Fair winds and safe dunes to you, Captain.' And at that he turned and sped off back to his frantic waiting.

A low whistle went out and Silvaran's crew jumped up, accompanying Der out of the food shop in tow of their captain. They swaggered down several more crudely shored up tunnels to another door that looked like a fridge. Captain Silvaran knocked twice, paused, then knocked three more times.

A gruff voice bellowed from behind, 'Name and password!'

'Silvaran,' he said sternly, then paused. 'To the furthest dunes and edges of night.'

Der heard a low grinding noise of several bolts and heavy objects being shifted from behind the door. Then the ancient fridge door opened to reveal, not the inside of a fridge, but a partially silhouetted figure.

He was thin, like all the others Der had seen here, but extremely tall and hunched over. Even in the gloom, Der could make out a rugged face full of scars. His left ear was missing and his one good eye was fixed on Silvaran and his crew. In his hand he held a large and rusty cutlass.

'Aha you old desert dog!' he exclaimed in recognition. 'Been many meals since we saw you last. Come in. Your usual provisions are ready. Would you be needing something for the young'un?'

Silvaran patted the man affectionately on the back and

said in his low and gruff voice, 'Yes, blankets and a hammock for her, Grogen!'

Grogen smiled a mischievous smile. 'Didn't take you for the nanny sort, old friend.'

Silvaran came back with sharp wit. 'No, but I hear the kindergarten you run here is the best around.'

The two of them broke out into a deep rumbling laughter. Grogen then let out a sharp whistle and at once a small team of men and women scurried around preparing provisions for Silvaran and his crew. Der peeped into room after room, that seemed to be filled with pirates and their crew sleeping or lounging.

At the end of the corridor, they were led into a larger, well-kept room. There were four hammocks hanging from the ceiling, a rug that appeared to have been woven from old fabric garments hanging on the wall and a small table in one corner.

'Just how you left it, Captain, as always. After you settle in, join me in my lounge to catch up on old times.'

'That would be good, Grogen,' Silvaran agreed, as the five of them strolled into their personal room.

'I think I am going to get a bit of shut eye, Cap, if that is OK,' said Slemp. The markings on his muscular arms twisted and turned and mesmerised Der, who told herself not to stare, but just couldn't help it. The patterns imitated plants of some description.

Slemp grinned at Der. 'Ah you ain't seen someone from Spin before, have you?' he said in a kind voice.

'Where is that?' Der asked.

'It is far beyond the other side of the forest, but many generations ago when the forest was much vaster, it was *on* the edge of the forest and my people lived and happily traded with the Virdarians.'

'It is quite difficult to get to nowadays,' Silvaran interjected. 'It takes the fastest ship and a more than reckless crew!'

'Ah that it does,' Slemp replied, a mist of nostalgia momentarily overtaking him, as he thought of something he seldom did – his homeland. Then almost as quickly he looked back over to Der.

'In Spin a child gets their first marking when they are ten, taking a perilous trip to the now distant forest. And then every time they visit the forest after that, they add a mark. It is a way to remind us of our respect and connection to the forest,' he said with a little pride.

Der took another long look at all the marks on Slemp's arm. 'How many perilous trips to the forest did you make?' she asked.

'Lots, but my last would have been the last anyone had seen of me, if it hadn't been for Silvaran here.'

'Ah, you would have found a way to survive!' Silvaran said dismissively. Slemp climbed into his hammock and yawned. 'Right, let's hit the lounge,' Silvaran said, leaving Slemp to rest.

The crew sat on a makeshift sofa made of old timber and fabric stuffed with forest moss. Der sat in the middle, with Arc on one side and the other crew member – Bline – on her other. Half asleep from the long journey, she could make out the sound of Silvaran and Grogen on the other side of the room, sipping cups of an odd liquid, deep in conversation. She gazed over and listened.

'Oh, I know, Cap, and what about that time we stripped the slaver's ship while they had stopped for supplies!' The two chuckled at each other, their eyes blurry with memories.

'Or the time you single-handedly took on the crew of the *Gizzard-Slasher* to win our bet.' Silvaran pointed to Grogen's rusty sword with a smile. 'Your sword was in far better nick then though; you could barely open a can of beans with it now!'

'Oh, never you mind about my blade, it could still take on three people and have room for their captain. Yours is not looking as sharp as in our sailing days either!'

Suddenly Der's eyes were wide open and she sat bolt upright. Silvaran had jumped to his feet in a blur and drawn his gleaming blade and Grogen was towering over him with his own great, but rather rusty blade.

Before Der could gasp in surprise the two swords were clashing in great clouts. The two aged men moved like young lions, lunging and parrying, shifting their feet this way and that like a delicate dance; a delicate but deadly dance.

'You're a little slow today, Captain Bronze!' Grogen taunted.

'And you would be better using that rusty old sword

of yours as a walking stick!' Captain Silvaran replied with wit just as fast as his blade. And so they went on, swords flashing, clanging together, only separated by even sharper retorts.

Arc noticed Der's white face and put a firm hand on her shoulder. 'Don't worry, they always do this!' she explained. 'They're the oldest of friends. Grogen was Silvaran's shipmate for most of his life. The two were a formidable force!'

Colour slowly returned to Der's face, and gradually she began to watch the two great pirates with awe and excitement, rather than shock and fear.

'Why did Grogen stop sailing?' Der asked, without taking her eyes off the spectacle.

'Ah, a while ago now Grogen wanted to settle down and retire. He used a tiny fraction of his spoils to set up this place,' Arc explained.

'He still seems deadly with that blade!' Der said in awe.

'Oh, he is. Only surpassed by Silvaran himself! One day I want to be as good as him,' Arc said with passion in her eyes.

She pushed her streak of sheer white hair out of her face, and Der observed her pale milky eyes, like those of the others she had met, yet hers were filled with fire.

'How did you join Silvaran's crew?' Der asked, drawn in by the romantic glamour of watching two great pirates jostle. Arc glanced at her fellow crew member Bline, fast asleep on the sofa.

'Silvaran is a bit of a hero where I come from, in Fringetown, but especially to my mother, who is a very old friend of Silvaran's. I'm not sure when or why they became friends, but whenever Silvaran was in town he would always make a thing of visiting her. I grew up hearing Silvaran's stories as a child.

'I think those stories got under my skin and by the time I was ten, I got it into my head that I had to join his crew and travel the barren deserts in search of danger, and nothing or no one, would stop me. I asked him if I could join, but he just laughed at me, much to my mother's relief. Most kids would have given up then and there, but it made me more determined, and every time he visited, I asked again, month in, month out. And every time he said no.'

'Did he say why?' Der asked, filled with curiosity.

'Too young, too weak, too short. And the list of reasons went on. But I kept on asking. At fifteen I packed some things, snuck onto his ship and stowed away. But we only got an hour out of Fringetown before he noticed and he dragged me back to my mother. They were both so angry and tried to educate me about the dangers of sailing the desert. My brother cried for days, worried he would never see me again. Silly boy!'

'Did you ever try stowing away on his ship again?' Der asked. 'After such a scolding?'

'Yeah, in the following few years, 139 more times, but each time he found me and dragged me back. And each time my worried mother, tearful brother and an angry

Silvaran gave me a scolding and lectures and even tried to distract my focus with other things. But I wouldn't give up.

'Eventually, fed up with being told I couldn't be a desert pirate, I packed my bag and simply ran away. I managed to get passage on a cargo ship that was scheduled to take salvaged material from Fringetown to Balldock. It was a hard journey and took almost a month, and the captain worked me so hard that I almost died of exhaustion and starvation. But eventually I arrived in Balldock, with a pocketknife, a few clothes and the hope of finding a ship that would let me join.'

'But Balldock, this place, looks really dangerous. Weren't you scared?' Der asked. Arc glanced at the sleeping crewmate to check again that he was still fast asleep and leaned in closer to Der.

'I don't know why I'm telling you this, I've never spoken about it to anyone before except Silvaran, but something about you, Der, makes me want to trust you, so I will continue. I thought I could take on the world with my pocketknife, but when I arrived I realised the dangerous reality of this place and yes, I was terrified. And like hungry animals, the evil here smelt my fear.

No sooner had I stepped off the transport ship, I was robbed at knife point by a gang called the Gulls. Then the trouble really began. When Silvaran said to you earlier, that this place is no place for a young'un, take my word for it, it isn't.

'Soon I joined a gang myself, just like the one that

robbed me, just to get a little food. But the gang eventually sold me to pirates as a slave. Alone and afraid in the dark hull of a ship, shoulder to shoulder with other poor wretches, destined to be used as free labour for felling trees, night in and night out, until our bodies broke and we would be left for dead.

'My life had taken a dive to the lowest in just a few months, filled with regret for not heeding Silvaran's and mother's warnings about the dangerous world. But no matter how strong my young heart and head was, the shackles and whip broke me.' Arc's rock-solid composure had slipped away, as a few rogue tears managed to escape her stern eyes.

Der listened on, half in horror and half in desire to know more. 'How did you escape?' she asked.

'A shiver of fear went down my spine that night as the ship lurched, casting off from Balldock and making its way up the slope, out to the desert. Behind me was my freedom and ahead darkness.

'I closed my eyes and tried to find solitude in the gentle sway of the hefty ship as it made its way towards the forest and our first night of hard labour. After several hours, though, the ship came to a sudden halt and we were all alarmed by a commotion and screams coming from above deck. Then it fell silent, a buzzing ominous silence, suddenly broken by the hatch to the hold being torn off and the silver moonlight shining down over the sad and lost faces around me.

'One by one we were led out to the cooler air of the

desert and our shackles were taken off. I had glimpses of the twisted faces of the pirates that enslaved us, as I stepped up over the deck, down to the desert and my early freedom. I was met by the last person I would have expected to see – Silvaran.

'Once the rest of the slaves had been freed and passage to Balldock arranged, Silvaran grabbed me by the arm and bundled me onto his ship. I was ashamed, but also relieved.

'He said nothing for the weeks all the way back to Fringetown. I was marched down to my mother who broke down in tears, along with my brother who my disappearance had hit the worst. They were all furious with me for running away, but were so relieved that I was alive, that they pretended I had never left and it was just a normal visit from Silvaran.

'Then after a few days at dinner Silvaran stood up and spoke, in a tone I have seldom heard him use before or since. He said, "Arc, do you still want to be a desert pirate?" I thought for a while, glimpsing the faces of my mother, Silvaran and my scatty brother Skoots. I felt guilty for upsetting and worrying them. But nothing had changed for me. I had learnt a hard lesson about going out into the world without being careful, but yes, I did still crave to be a pirate.

'So I looked Silvaran square in the eye and said simply, "Yes". He looked a little surprised given the ordeal I had been through. "Is there anything I can do or say," he asked, "that will stop you from running away, or trying to stow away on another ship?" I said "No", firmly.

'Silvaran turned to my mother and said, "Well if she keeps running away and won't at least wait until she is older, then the only thing for it is to let her join my crew. At least that way I can protect her and we will always know where she is!" And that's how I joined Silvaran, and I've enjoyed every moment of it so far!'

'Wow, what an awesome story of determination,' Der said with a spark of zest in her eye.

The two girls realised that Silvaran and Grogen were still fighting and turned back to watch. Finally, after a long and tiring sword fight that would have left most people exhausted ages ago, Silvaran parried a great blow from Grogen's rusty sword, jumped into the air, side-stepped Grogen and slapped him square on the leg with the flat of his blade. The two slumped to the floor in fits of laughter.

'Almost had you, Silvaran,' Grogen said between guffaws.

'You were not even close!' Silvaran replied, setting them off into fits of even greater laughter, which rumbled through the rooms and corridors of the pirate inn. Eventually they returned to their drinks and reminiscing.

Der listened long into the morning, their stories igniting her imagination further. She finally drifted off to sleep a little before midday.

CHAPTER TEN

When Der awoke, she was in a soft hammock in the crew's room. Great snoring came from the other hammocks and far off in the corner she could just make out Silvaran sleeping like a baby; even asleep he was stony calm. She dozed off again, her ears adjusting to the surrounding loud musical snores.

The next time she awoke, she was rudely pulled out of a dream, where she was captain of her own desert ship. She opened her eyes, to see one of Slemp's patterned arms shaking her and softly whispering, 'Time to go, missy. The sun will set in a few minutes; we can't waste a moment of the night!'

Der felt a little disorientated by the nocturnal life in the desert. Reluctantly, she got herself together and was soon following Silvaran back down the corridors, having said goodbye to Grogen.

As they came back out into the open expanse of Balldock, she was no longer timid. She strolled, almost swaggered, mimicking the rest of the crew. Soon they had made their way through the bustle of the waking dock, and they were boarding their ship.

They readied the ship and on Silvaran's command a group of dockhands surrounded the *Dawn Eagle*. They all took hold and to Der's amazement they pushed the ship towards the entrance of the stadium. When they got there, a hook was attached to the prow of the ship. A tall man by the entrance gave Silvaran a wink and pulled a lever.

'Hold on tight, Der!' Silvaran bellowed. She grabbed onto the closest thing just in time, as suddenly there was a giant twang and a bungee cord catapulted the ship back up the tunnel and finally out into the cool early evening air.

The first signs of the moon and stars broke the hazy dusk. A whistle filled the air, and the crew went to work. The sails billowed out as the early night wind hit them and they were soon cruising back through the desert dunes, the glowing lamp on the bow lighting their way.

Der was filled with excitement as she watched the greasy early evening darkness little by little awake with the glows of other ships. Silvaran strode past Der, then with the agility of a cat, leapt up, grabbed a dangling rope and shimmied up it, faster than a monkey. Der could just make out the captain chatting to Arc, way up the mast.

'We will be heading across the Snake Fields, then on towards The Fringeland Flats. Keep a sharp eye out, Arc,' Silvaran said in his low gravelly voice.

'Always, Cap, always. Are we lure dropping as we go, Cap?' Arc asked with a glint in her eye.

'It would be rude to turn down the snakes' hospitality!' Silvaran said and the two chuckled. 'Oh, and one more thing, Arc,' he said in a serious tone. 'Word is, sightings of the Fulgur seem to be on the increase, so keep a sharp eye out.'

Arc looked a little fearful at the mention of the beast, but before she could reply, Silvaran had stepped off the edge, caught one of the dangling ropes and slid back to the deck in a split second. He sent out a series of low bursts of whistles and the ship changed course.

Der settled down on the helm close to Silvaran, watching the flashes of dunes speed by, and the grey evening sky become a rich velvet black. As the early evening flew by, almost as fast as their ship, Der became aware that the further they travelled the fewer ships there were, till they were the only glowing light she could make out in any direction.

'Captain,' she whispered softly, to avoid disturbing or startling him.

'Yes, missy,' Silvaran replied, without taking his eyes off the horizon for a moment.

'I've noticed that the further we sailed tonight, the less we come across other ships. Are we leaving civilisation?' Der enquired.

'Ah, for such young inexperienced eyes you are observant. We are taking a seldom travelled route across the Wastelands to the furthest point of known civilisation. A place called the Fringetown. It usually takes many weeks to get there, but we are taking a shortcut across the Snake Fields, then the Cockroaches' Lair and finally on through the grey pass. We will make it in just shy of three days!'

Der let her imagination run wild for a moment at the names of the places Silvaran had mentioned, till a question stopped her daydream abruptly.

'But why do the other ships not take this route?' she asked, almost hoping the answer was not what she suspected.

Silvaran bellowed out in a great laugh. 'Well, missy, very few captains are brave or stupid enough to take such a route. The very few pirates, trade ships and explorers that are destined for Fringetown, take The Dune Tracks instead.'

Der slunk down to the deck in a panic. Momentarily Silvaran took his eyes off the horizon. 'Don't worry, Der, we know this route and the perils it provides. I have to be back in Balldock in a week to meet an explorer who wants safe passage to the Glass Fields. So, we ride the Snake Fields,' Silvaran said as he patted Der on the back. 'Trust us!' he whispered as he turned back to the wheel and the horizon.

The air cooled the further into the night that they travelled and little by little the dunes flattened to great vast plains of sand. Just then Arc called out, 'Approaching the Snake Fields, Cap!'

Silvaran responded by tightening his grip on the wheel and sharpening his gaze ahead. Der's curiosity led her to find a spot that she could take a good look from. Gazing over the side in the dim orange glow of the ship's light, she could just make out what looked like small holes all over the sandy landscape.

She strained her eyes with excitement and curiosity when she heard Arc shout, 'Knots approaching!' At first there was nothing, but the dusty dry wasteland with a scattering of holes. Then off in the distance, quickly approaching, she saw a slow and lazy area of something like rope twisting and turning into knots.

The closer they got, the more agitated the knotted area became, till it began to writhe and shift, like a pool or ocean. Suddenly there were bangs and crashes coming from under the ship. Der looked directly down to see that the agitated knots were in fact hundreds of snakes, that had been rudely awoken by the ship.

She squinted to see where the snakes ended, but to her great surprise, she could not see an end. She looked back and already the *Dawn Eagle*'s tracks had been filled back in again by a great writhing entity of snakes. The bangs got louder, and even Silvaran looked a little on edge by the sheer numbers of the snakes that night. Der gasped as she realised there were snakes wriggling on other snakes, like a great sea, apparently endless in all directions.

'This place is called the Snake Fields because for some reason there is an abundance of snakes that live in these flat wastelands,' Silvaran explained. 'No one knows what they eat, or what sustains so many, but every night when the sun goes down and the air begins to chill, they gather together in their millions to keep warm. They are docile and slow in the cold of the night, but they can still be whipped up into a frenzy. No matter what, we cannot stop! If we did, they would engulf us immediately and strip us to the bone.'

Der looked away in horror. The bangs grew louder followed by jolts. Silvaran set out a series of short whistles, and the 'V' sails opened and fluttered. He pulled a small lever next to him and the lights on the ship brightened, awakening the snakes which rapidly began to slither away to safety.

Der spun round at the sound of a rope behind her being dropped. The rope was brightly coloured and bounced and jumped along the dirt behind them. After a short while Der had to look forward in order to avoid feeling sick. She held on tightly and gritted her teeth, enduring the speed and violence of their movement.

What felt an eternity passed, slowly and uncomfortably for Der. The only thing that kept her rooted to the spot, tensely grasping the ship, was the thought of falling over the side into the depths of the snake sea.

Hours later, when the ship slowed to its usual central mast speed, Der was shivering cold and as white as snow. Her fingers had seized up around the railing that she had hung on to. Her legs were spasming in fear and cold. Tears were streaming down her face. She felt a warm and kind arm on her shoulder. It was Slemp.

'It is OK now, missy, we are through the Snake Fields. You can let go now; you are safe.'

Bline also came over with a warm blanket, which he draped over Der without exchanging a word. They both spent a while reassuring her and making sure that she was warm.

'Take a rest for a while, missy, we will be at the whistling caves soon enough, where we can rest for the day, eat and recover.' Der drifted off into a shallow sleep, exhausted by the ordeal.

She dreamt of things that seemed strangely familiar, yet also completely alien. Cars and city streets, people bustling around in a rush to get to places; she was standing in the middle of it all, being buffeted by all the passers-by.

The shaking grew more, and suddenly Der herd Bline's voice. 'Wake up, missy, the sun will come up soon. Wake up!'

Der opened her eyes, to see Silvaran and his crew lowering the gangplank at the base of a rock that jutted out of the surrounding wastelands. They helped Der to her feet, off the ship and up an ancient crudely cut path that meandered towards the top of the cliff.

It was difficult to see in the dim glow of their electric lamps, but as they climbed, the first glimmers of the morning sunlight spilt over the horizon, basking the rock in fiery oranges. A little way up, they reached a small entrance. Inside was a fairly large cave with some crude seating, bedding and a firepit. Bline was the last to enter the cave and he dragged a sack behind him.

'Sup time,' he said in a subdued voice. Slemp was already making a small fire in the pit, a long knife resting close to his leg. Bline hurried to the fire area and slumped the sack down. It hit the ground with a thud and out of it rolled a dead snake. It was as long as Der and as wide as Silvaran's leg.

The crew got to work on what looked like a well-practised routine. One trimming and cleaning off the scales, another top and tailing it, and another dicing it into steaks. Arc rummaged around in the assortment of objects in the cave and dragged over a large sheet of metal, which she placed over the fire. Der watched in surprise as the crew placed the steaks on the fire and seasoned them with a variety of herbs.

'Are you going to eat snake?' Der said in horror. The crew fell silent for a moment and looked at Der's horrified face.

'Too right we are going to eat it!' Arc said licking her lips. A rumble of 'Lovely snake steaks' came from the crew.

'But isn't it poisonous?' Der asked in surprise.

Silvaran stepped forward to explain. 'We used a lure as we sailed the snake sea, Der. This is a lock snake, unlike lots of them it doesn't use venom, instead, it bites down hard on its prey, locking its jaw and writhes around till its prey is exhausted. But it has just bitten off more than it could chew! It makes unbelievable steaks. So good, traversing the Snake Fields is almost worth the trouble!'

Soon the soft and mouth-watering aromas were snaking around the air. Der could not resist; it did smell delicious. By the time that Slemp announced that the steaks were ready, Der was the first one to tuck in.

It was a rich oily meat, full of flavour. And the best thing that Der had tasted in – well, as long as she could remember, which for her was not actually that long! As soon as they had finished cooking the meat, they put out the small fire.

The soft glows of orange light soon turned to a bright sunlight that lit the entrance of the cave so brightly that the crew hung a piece of old fabric over the small opening. Above the firepit was a shaft that vented the smoke. Now as the temperature rose outside, the vent created a constant cooling breeze.

Der and the crew lay back on the soft bedding mats, with full and contented stomachs, letting the gentle breeze cool them. Soon one by one they drifted off to sleep.

Suddenly Der awoke, hot and uncomfortable, a noise breaking into her dreams that had been of odd places in which people used to keep books. There was a low and undulating whistle that, though it was not loud, was just audible enough to disturb her sleep.

The sound reverberated around the cave. Looking round in fear, Der's imagination began to run amok. Was it a wolf, or a bear, or worse – the Fulgur? She took a deep breath and tried to analyse the possible source of the noise, till she fell back and discreetly chuckled to herself. 'The whistling caves, that's why they're called that,' she muttered. Soon the warm breeze and the musical whistling lulled her back off to sleep.

It was early evening before anyone stirred again. As the last sunny tide went out and disappeared over the horizon, Der rubbed her eyes and glanced around at her newfound companions all stirring and waking up for another day, or, rather, night.

Soon the fire was lit, and they were tucking into a hearty breakfast of the other half of the snake and drinking an odd tea-like liquid they called bristle vine infusion. Der knew better than to ask what was in it though, as by now she had realised that sometimes it is just better to not know what you are eating or drinking!

And as the first signs of a crisp clear night sky emerged, they made their way back down to the tethered desert ship, the *Dawn Eagle.*

CHAPTER ELEVEN

Arc stood on the prow in the light of the moons, excitement in her eyes and one hand resting on the pommel of her sword. Slemp and Bline looked poised ready for their captain's orders. Even Der stood a little taller, surrounded by her friends, looking forward to the dangers and adventures that the next sail might hold. Silvaran stood at the wheel, finely dressed, with his tricorn hat and a glint in his eye.

'OK, crew, you know what comes next. Make sure you watch all sides of the ship and keep your weapons at the ready,' he said, with a hint of excitement in his voice and the tiniest of smiles in the corner of his mouth.

'Captain, could I help out?' Der pluckily asked. The tiny smile in the corner of Silvaran's mouth grew by a few more fractions and he turned to Der.

'It will be dangerous, Der. You might be better off below deck. The Cockroaches' Lair is a formidable place and its people are a ruthless and lawless kind that take pleasure in attacking and killing everyone that passes.'

Der straightened up and spoke boldly. 'You are all risking your lives to take me to safety; I'm not going anywhere. Please give me a task, Cap.'

Silvaran looked fractionally surprised by Der's sudden determination. 'Oh, alright, Der, but if the fighting gets really bad, I will ask you to take cover below. Take these!' he said in a stern voice.

He reached down to the many objects that hung from his thick leather belt and plucked two items which he held out. She took them from his hand and inspected them with sparkling eyes. One was a section of old pipe with makeshift lenses fitted and the other was a rough-cut wooden catapult.

'Right, Slemp, you man the forecastle!' he bellowed. 'Bline, take the portside centre and, Der, you take starboard. Arc, use the height to your advantage and I will hold the aft castle.'

Bline took Der to the central area of the ship and briefed her. He spoke softly, 'Keep your eyes out over there, Der. Here are the sand balls for your pult; don't let the 'Roaches' get close to the ship. Have you ever used a pult before?' he asked gently.

As Der inspected the device, it reminded her of a cruder version of Golderwin's catapult. 'Yes, I should be OK,' she said, trying to sound confident.

Bline bent down and showed Der how to load and pull back the pult. He pointed to a small boulder about halfway up the rockface and with a loud twang let it go. The sand ball whizzed through the air and thudded into the boulder, exploding into a cloud of dust when it impacted.

'Now you try, Der,' he said.

Der loaded the pult with the grainy sand ball, strained it back and let go. The ball whizzed through the air, missing the boulder completely. Der looked a little frustrated and tried again. The ball narrowly missed the boulder this time. It was a little different than the pult Golderwin had, but after several more attempts, she got used to it and on her final attempt, hit the boulder precisely where Bline had.

Bline looked a little surprised and muttered, 'Beginner's luck,' then strode off to the port side.

Moments later Silvaran's whistle cracked the calm dusk night and the sails billowed out into action. The deft craft rode the breeze like its namesake. Soon they were travelling across a wide valley of flat sandy plains broken up by a smattering of protruding boulders.

Der could feel her heart pumping, her eyes constantly glued to the starboard horizon, scanning around constantly for those Cockroaches.

'Mustn't let them get close,' she muttered to herself. Her other hand was firmly on her pult. Around her waist hung a pult belt, that Bline had let her borrow. It was made of an old section of hide, with a large offset open pouch to put the sand balls in. Der could feel the weight of them on her right side. Unlike the crew, she was left-handed, which they had all found a novelty when she strapped on the pult belt.

She could feel the adrenalin pumping through her body, heightening her awareness. By the time the first sign of movement had been spotted, though, she had already been staring out poised for an attack for hours and was beginning to wonder if there really was anything dangerous out there.

As she rested her elbow on the railings and let the pult hang loosely in her hand beside her waist, there was a tiny glint from one of the distant boulders, then another.

Arc sent out a shrill whistle, and at once everyone straightened up, poised for battle. Bline had already loaded his pult and lined up more sand balls on the railings ready. He narrowed his eyes, like a leopard about to pounce.

Der noticed a few more glints. Then all of a sudden, a loud battle cry rang out, immediately followed by several tiny craft emerging from behind boulders.

The crafts were far, far smaller than the *Dawn Eagle*. Swift and agile, they meandered and encircled the ship. On board each one, there were two figures, with barely enough space to move. The driver sat on a small crate, while the other stood in the back behind a makeshift turret woven together out of twisted metal, rope and wood.

Around the top of each turret were sharp spikes. The figures were all dressed in black, wearing rounded leather helmets with various spikes and horns. Their eyes were a little less milky than most of the people Der had met, but they stared with crazed violent looks. Their faces were crudely painted with red pigment, many of them pierced with pieces of chain or other assortments of objects.

They buzzed around the *Dawn Eagle* like piranhas swarming prey. For a moment, there was a pause, a silent suspense. Then louder than anything Der could remember hearing, the Cockroaches cried out a blood-curdling cry, shaking a concoction of sharp homemade weapons high above their heads. And then there was a pause, as though awaiting a response. Away in the distance a massive ship slowly rumbled towards them.

Der could make out a tall woman, her face completely covered in piercings, shimmering in the moon light. As the rumbling ship edged closer, Der realised the gigantic ship was not powered by sails at all. Instead, there were eight Virdarians in chains all rotating hand cranks attached to a mechanical system of belts that drove the wheels. Darting around the tall slaves were several people, whipping and lashing out.

The tall lady high up on top of the ship held up a sword, and brought it down in a swoop with a bloodcurdling scream of fury, much to her subjects' delight.

Silvaran gasped as he noticed the leader's ship and the poor forest slaves powering it. A great twang of pults being released added to the noisy chaos. A driver got hit square in the face by Slemp, knocking him off his perch. Instantly the small craft hurtled out of control into another, sending both crafts into rolls and scattering the three crew onto the soft sand.

Silvaran dashed over to a large monopod mounted catapult in the aft castle and with great 'vhooms' let fly a series of larger sand balls, which slammed into the turrets of two more Cockroach crafts, smashing the crude constructions into a flurry of pieces. The two crafts veered off and sped away.

While Silvaran and his crew reloaded, however, a haphazard flurry of small lumps of steel, plastic and sand balls collided with the *Dawn Eagle*.

Der and the crew dropped down behind the protective railings, as the shards rained down on the ship like a hailstorm. A whistle signalled the crew to jump back up and return fire.

Der felt determination surge through her veins like fire. She pulled back her pult, took careful aim and hit one of the craft drivers square between the eyes, sending him flying. The craft hit a rock and flipped over, but by then she had already reloaded and was firing again.

This time she hit another driver in the hand. He let go of the wheel in a panic, and it rolled over in a pile of dust.

Another fear-gripping cry went up from the Cockroach leader as they sailed in closer to the *Dawn Eagle*. A flurry of projectiles shot back in answer from the *Dawn Eagle*'s crow's nest, thumping into the figures on board the tiny crafts. Five more crude vessels rolled, flipped, and crashed into piles of scrap. But more came to fill their places.

A cry came from the Cockroaches as they sent

another deadly bombardment towards the *Dawn Eagle*. Crashes and shattering sounds filled the air. Der's ears were ringing. She and most of the crew managed to duck down behind the railings.

Then Der glanced over to see that Bline had been hit in the chest by a shard of rusty metal. His leather coat had helped to take some of the impact. But as he knelt on the deck with both hands grasping his chest, she saw a small trickle of blood.

Another whistle rang out and Der focused on protecting the ship, while fighting the urge to run over and help Bline. When Der looked back over the side, the sight struck fear into her heart.

The tiny crafts had surrounded the ship and the rear riders were throwing up grappling hooks. They stuck fast into the railings. Der watched in horror as the spike-clad Cockroaches climbed the ropes.

'Der, cut 'em down!' Silvaran bellowed as he slid a knife over to her. Der grabbed the knife and began working away at the thick rope. When the figure realised, he sped up, trying to get to the railings before the rope was severed. But Der was too fast.

With a twang, the man dropped away, still holding the rope, a mixture of surprise and anger in his eyes. Others dropped away too, all round the ship, as the crew darted this way and that.

But more and more came, and while they worked in a frenzy, flitting all over to cut down the grappling hooks, the numbers just kept coming.

The first of the Cockroaches jumped over the railings and drew a deadly looking serrated blade. Rage and bloodlust in his eyes, he swung the heavy blade towards Slemp, flailing it around in a display of raw strength.

Slemp drew his own curved blade and took a step back into a warlike stance, the markings on his arm shimmering in the moonlight as he shifted and moved out of the way of the Cockroach's slow cleaving arcs. His eyes narrowed waiting for his moment. As the man finished a large slash, Slemp sidestepped the figure and brought the hilt of his sword deftly down on the unsuspecting man's back, sending him tumbling off balance. Falling head over heels over the railings he landed on his craft driver below, creating another pile of chaotic scrap.

Five more figures appeared at the aftcastle, all swinging an assortment of barbaric weapons. In a flash Silvaran was there in front of them. Eerie grins filled the Cockroaches' faces as they inspected the old captain. But before they could lift their swords for their first blows, Silvaran was upon them: parrying, dodging, ducking.

One caught an elbow in the side, another felt a swift foot take their feet away from under them, another two were kicked over the side and the last, well let's just say… he got the point!

Meanwhile the bow of the ship was being overrun too. Twenty or so of them stood there, smirks of victory on their faces, as Silvaran and his crew drew back to defend the aftcastle.

Der suddenly had an idea. She dashed below deck, only to reappear moments later next to Silvaran and his crew. To the amazement of both groups, Der boldly stepped forward towards the Cockroaches. She drew back her pult.

A booming and crazed laugh went up from the figures as they stared down at the girl who appeared to be single-handedly challenging them.

One particularly large gruesome man stepped forward, adorned in plastic and metal foraged items. A long razor hung from his ear and his face was a railroad of scars. One eye was covered by a makeshift patch made from an old bottle cap, covering a battle wound that surely had cost him his eye.

He drew his sharp serrated sword and advanced steadily, his unflinching gaze fixed on Der as he stared down the stretched aiming elastic of the pult.

Silvaran and his crew rushed forward to protect Der. The Cockroaches let out a battle roar. There was a twang.

CHAPTER TWELVE

Silvaran and his crew came to, with cloudy heads. 'I don't remember hitting the grog wine last night, lads?' Silvaran said as he glanced around with bleary eyes, struggling to take in his surroundings.

He was slumped on the aftcastle next to his other crew members and he glanced at them each in turn, taking stock of the situation. The deck was in a state, cracked, splintered, stained with blood, and strewn with an assortment of debris.

He swivelled round to look at the helm. There, as bold as brass, was a cheeky girl standing at the wheel. Standing at *his* wheel. Of *his* ship. And what was more she was wearing *his* hat! He sifted his memories, till a few fragments began to spark a name…

'Der,' he muttered. Silvaran's crew were also peering around, trying to piece together an explanation. Silvaran's stern face twisted through a variety of expressions till it settled on a particularly angry gaze. His eyebrows touched in the middle above his nose and his eye began to twitch.

'DER, HOW DARE YOU! NO ONE CAPTAINS

MY SHIP WITHOUT MY PERMISSION! AND HOW DARE YOU TOUCH MY HAT! Crew, prepare the plank and hoist the 'V' sail. She is going to take a walk.'

Loud panting came from the front of the ship and moments later Arc arrived at the captain's side.

'Cap, please calm down,' Arc said in a soft and respectful tone. 'Der saved us all with magic dust. You will feel groggy for a while. I let her sail the ship while I kept the sails plump and started to navigate us through the grave of a thousand ships.'

Silvaran appeared to calm down but demanded to know how they escaped the Cockroaches. 'Der used some magic dust and they all slept, along with you, Captain!' Arc said.

'I've told you it isn't magic, Arc,' said Der. 'It's simply sleepy dust, from a plant in the forest. Arc was high up in the crow's nest, so didn't get hit. But those Cockroaches all dropped like flies. We tossed them over the side and Arc and I kept the ship moving in case they woke up.'

Silvaran's crew looked perplexed that a girl could have single-handedly taken on the entire swarm of Cockroaches. Just then there was a small bump as the ship hit something. Der rushed back to the helm to steer the ship and Arc rushed to help her.

Rising up high above the *Dawn Eagle* were half covered wrecks of ships. The wood and metal had been bleached by the intense sun and sand-blasted by the winds. Shiny patches marked areas that the wind had polished. They were shells, skeletons of once grand ships, stripped clean of anything that might be of value and left to be savaged by the brutal desert. Tatters of their once grand sails flapped from their masts. Der watched each one as they passed through the narrow channels between wreck after wreck.

'What is this place?' Der asked. Silvaran stood, and lethargically walked up to the helm. He snatched his hat off Der's head.

'Now let's get one thing straight, Der, a man's hat is his pride and joy, almost as important as his ship!' Silvaran placed the hat back on his own head and tried to take the wheel, still squinting.

After several tries, he gave up and leant against the railings, using them to hold himself up. 'Second thought, Der, you take the helm for now. I don't feel quite right.'

His crew were not much better either, they had all sustained a heavy dose of sleepy dust when Der had pulted the Cockroaches with it.

'Sorry, Captain,' Der said sheepishly. 'I shouldn't have taken your hat. I guess I got a bit carried away and needed to shield the moon's gaze from my eyes.'

She felt hot and flushed as she realised that Silvaran's stern gaze was a hundred per cent on her. She hung her head, while the crew remained absolutely silent, trying to fathom out their captain's next move.

The silence grew and wrapped around the ship, as everyone on board, especially Der, worried about

Silvaran's sudden anger. You could hear a pin drop and hearts pounding, when out of nowhere Silvaran let out a great booming laugh that rattled around the ship and bounced its way across the ghost ships. Der breathed out with a small sigh.

'I am not saying that you should have taken care of the Roaches – we would have won anyway – or that your actions were right, Der, but I admire your bravery,' he said in a deep gravelly voice. 'But… If you touch my hat again, I will personally see to it that you are snake food!' His stony stare bored into Der's eyes.

Arc leant over and discreetly whispered in Der's ear,

'You did great, lass, thank you for saving our hides.' Silvaran looked back towards Der and gave her the tiniest of grins.

'Suits you, you know, the pirating life! This place is the heart of Roach country. Each one of these ships is a trophy taken by the Roaches. Attacked, boarded, the crews slaughtered and the ships stripped of every last thing. Very few ships pass this way now,' Silvaran explained.

He gave a shrill whistle, which was answered by two crew members all rushing groggily to their posts. Bline limped and staggered to his position, a large bandage around his chest covering the wound he had sustained by the attack.

Silvaran's eyes suddenly widened as he remembered an important detail. 'That large ship with the Roach leader. Tell me it didn't get away, Arc,' he said with wide sharp eyes.

'Captain, I am sorry they did get away. No sooner than they saw the Roaches' defeat, they turned about and fled,' Arc said in a low voice.

'There were forest slaves on board that ship. Which way did they sail?' Silvaran asked raising one eyebrow.

'Towards the Barren mountains, Captain,' Arc said swiftly.

'Well noted, Arc. Right, we need to get Der to safety double time and then return to find those slaves and free them!'

The crew, including Arc, looked shocked at the idea. Slemp tentatively asked, 'Captain, you know we would follow you anywhere. But why would you want to risk such a perilous mission for the sake of a few forest people, not even people of our kind?'

Silvaran propped himself up straighter on the railings and adjusted his hat. 'The forest people and our people might not have always got along; they might have different views, but they are people, just like us. Their lives are worth just the same as ours, and besides, how could I look my dear old friend Golderwin in the eye again, if I didn't sail out and save 'em!'

His crew looked quite moved and surprised by their captain's strength and compassionate words. He continued, 'I know that many would not risk their lives to save a forester, and I know that sailing into the heart of Cockroach country, defeating or outsmarting them and freeing their slaves, before getting away alive is a bold, and some might say suicidal, mission. So I would only ask those of you that know the risks and want to accompany me to come. Who stands with me?' he roared.

Four thundering shouts went up as Bline, Slemp, Arc and even Der stepped forward, raised their weapons and bellowed out, 'I do!'

Silvaran spun round to Der. 'Sorry, Der, not you. Not this adventure. It has been fun to see your bravery and have you aboard, but I promised I would get you to Fringetown and safety. And my word is my bond!'

Der stepped back, disappointed at not being allowed to come on such a rescue. 'But…' she began, but Silvaran's cold hard stare was on her and she knew that she would be a fool to challenge him on this in front of his crew. He had only just got over the 'hat' business, after all.

Silvaran's hand fell firmly on her shoulder. 'You are a brave one, Der. You will make a great pirate, one day, if that is your desire. But not now and not yet,' he said with a small smile.

As they left the last of the ghost ships and their eerie reminders of the savage Cockroaches behind, the 'V' sail went up and they cruised through the dusky Barren Wasteland.

They travelled all through the night, and just as the early hours of the next morning were marked by a sky washed with an orange haze, Der could make out the silhouette of a large structure in the distance, jutting out of the sand, and beyond it, a gorge that ran between two rocky plateaus.

By the time they had reached the structure, the first fingers of the morning sun were tickling the desert dunes. Der gazed up in amazement, as they passed under the giant edifice.

It was made of a grey stone-like material. Cracks ran the length and breadth of it and brown rust-runs stained the stone like blood. Twisted metal reinforcements marked areas where the grey stone had crumbled away. The sides of the structure had been sheared off and metal was hanging out like entrails. As they swooped under it, they came into a shadowy gorge. The ever-blazing heat of the desert sun seemed not to make it down in the gorge. A musty damp smell drifted in the stagnant air.

They slowed back to the normal sails. With a tiny whistle the ship's lights brightened. Der had been gently relieved of her place at the helm just before they had entered the gorge.

Silvaran stood back at the helm, pulling levers and wrestling with the wheel, to keep enough wind in the sails to move forward and navigate through the twisting, meandering narrow route.

The exhaustion of the battle and Der's long night began to hit her, when she finally slumped down against the mast. Almost instantly she felt the adrenalin and excitement that had kept her awake and alert fizzle away.

She drifted off to sleep almost instantly, not to awake for nearly thirteen hours.

When she did awake, it was to a similar sight. They were sailing along a narrow route with steep rocky cliffs veering up either side. The track was bumpy and only just wide enough for the ship. The last light of the day barely made it that far into the steep valley, and the same damp air hung around.

'Welcome back, Der. Come up here!' Silvaran said in a cheerful tone. Der jumped up, feeling a new energy after her long sleep and rushed to the helm where the captain stood in his dapper clothing. His eyes looked tired and red, as he peered down at Der.

'See how I pull the corresponding lever as we go round the sharp turns in the gorge. The left and right levers operate simple brakes that help us manoeuvre tightly round the turns. Here, you have a go, lass!'

Der hesitantly took hold of the wheel, not knowing if she was really allowed.

'Grip the wheel tight, Der, ships need to be kept under control. And just like wild creatures, they will smell your fear!' He let out a series of booming laughs and boldly strode down the steps towards the lower decks.

Der let out a little gasp when she realised that Silvaran had left her alone to sail the ship and appeared to be off to the hammock room below deck. But she got a grip of her fear and felt that old friend of hers, that had seen her through so many a scrape, more than she could even remember: determination! She stood straight, rolled back her shoulders, narrowed her eyes and concentrated on keeping the ship gliding smoothly around the meandering track.

Just as Der heard the last of Silvaran's heavy boots step off the last rung of the stairs below deck, there was a short whistle. Arc slid down the mast in a display of debonair and disappeared below deck, only to reappear next to Der holding a dusty, shabby old bicorn hat.

'Cap wanted you to have this, missy. Seems you made quite an impression on him, by singlehandedly taking on the Cockroaches and sailing his ship, despite being only a young'un! But don't tell him that I said that to you. Cap doesn't like to hand out compliments,' Arc said with a huge grin.

Before Der could reply, she had shimmied back up the mast to her favourite spot in the crow's nest. Der carefully placed the dusty bicorn hat on her head, took a strong grip of the wheel and with a smile from ear to ear, she wound the ship through the valley like a needle. Over the next few hours, each one of Silvaran's crew discreetly came up and patted her on the back, whispering, 'Thanks, Der.'

She sailed deep and long into the following night, till she could make out the tiny traces of the sunrise, way, way up above, refusing to venture down into the gorge.

The night had sped by quickly, with the excitement and honour of sailing a desert ship. And not just any ship, but the infamous *Dawn Eagle*. Der felt a rough pat on the back and turning to see who it was, saw a refreshed and wide-awake Captain Silvaran towering over her.

'Well done, missy, a smooth night's sailing. You are a natural! I mean for a young'un!'

Der smiled. 'Thank you, Captain. She is a truly magnificent ship!'

'That she is, missy. That she is! Derwin, you will find a comfy hammock set up downstairs in the small storeroom. Get some rest and if you like you can take the helm again later.'

Der strolled down to the lower deck. Just off from the main bunk room, the crew had prepared the storeroom for her. The room was bare, mostly made from old, reclaimed pieces of thin timber.

She climbed up into the welcoming hammock and as the ship gently sped on, the hammock wobbled and swayed from side to side. She was exhausted, but also could hardly wait till she could sail the *Dawn Eagle* again.

It was some time before they emerged from the monotonous deep gorge. By then their eyes had adapted to the constant dim light of it during the day. It was like a twilight valley, where the light seldom increased beyond a lazy dull eerie glow.

At last the ship emerged from the valley mouth and sped out across The Fringeland Flats. After so long in the gloom, the sheer brightness of the moon felt like an unbearable blinding glow. It was a while before their eyes adapted to the light, but when they did, Der was welcomed by a wonderful sight. The Fringeland Flats were vast, stretching out to the horizon in every direction.

'This looks like the safest part of our journey,' Der said in relief.

'The flats are indeed easy sailing,' Silvaran confirmed. 'But they are so truly vast and devoid of any landmarks, that many a seasoned sailor has become lost in them. Fringetown is a tiny point in a mammoth sea of flats. One degree out, and you could sail right past it without knowing. You will find no monsters or violent clans here, but running out of water and food are your enemies, or finding yourself out on the plains with no shelter in the daytime, where the sun will cook you alive in minutes! But don't worry, we have sailed the plains many a time. We have even been to the very edge of everything and back!' he said with a mixture of menace and adventure in his voice.

Der sat on the deck between duties of taking the helm. They whistled across the plains full speed, constantly adjusting course by a fraction or two.

CHAPTER THIRTEEN

It was late that night, when Arc shouted down from her lookout spot, 'Fringetown approaching!' a thrill of excitement in her voice.

'Excellent, Arc!' Silvaran replied. 'Can you stay back and ready the ship to leave, then meet us at your mum's?'

'Will do, Cap, we have some Roach hunting to do!' Arc replied with excitement.

'That we do!' Silvaran bellowed out, then made small adjustments to the wheel and let out a series of small whistles which were immediately acted upon by his crew.

Before Der could take stock of it all, they were dropping the sails and pulling up to a small round turret in the otherwise relentless empty plains. It looked like a large well, constructed from metal, a dark brown-red from years of rust.

The ship gracefully slid to a stop. Without wasting a moment, Bline was dropping the gangplank and Silvaran led the way around the circular structure. The sand was fine and compacted, offering no resistance, and off in the distance they saw a dust-devil idly playing in the wilderness of the plains.

As they approached the other side of the turret, Der could just make out a large metal door with round studs running down its height and length, each one with a rusty tear mark. To Der they looked like a hundred eyes.

Silvaran clenched his fist and rapped sternly on the door, his knocks tapping out a tune. Immediately afterwards a small peep-door slid open, just big enough for one person to look through. The look-hole had metal bars, similar to a prison cell door.

Der could just make out in the subdued dull light inside, a large man with a great round beard, that looked like he had got his head caught in a candy floss machine! Beyond the beard, Der could only make out the man's eyes and mouth, the rest of his facial features were lost, possibly forgotten!

'WHO GOES THERE?' the great man bellowed.

'From the furthest dunes and edges of night!' Silvaran answered.

There was a momentarily awkward silence, then the sound of steel bolts rang out in the otherwise silent and dead plains. The door swung open, and the man stepped out into the moonlight.

His beard was patchy in colour; orange with a hint of grey, and took up three times the space of his head, running all the way down to his waist. From beneath it, two kind but stern eyes shone.

He stepped towards Silvaran with great open arms, and much to Silvaran's embarrassment, gave him a giant full hug. Silvaran was engulfed by the man, but most of all by his beard.

'Silvaran, you old dog, been a long time since you visited your bro!' the orange-bearded man said in a deep and gravelly voice.

Just then Der gasped, covering her mouth with her hands, as she noticed that the man had a peg leg, made from an old hand-shaped piece of salvaged wood. The wood had the letters 'SS P' engraved on it. Der could not help but staring.

'Ahhh you like mi leg, young one,' he said. 'Lost it in a mining accident decades ago; mi new one is made from the remains of a famous real sailing ship from ancient times.'

'This is my younger brother Glime,' Silvaran chirped in, gesturing to Der. 'Der here was found wandering in the Last Forest. I promised to bring her to safety and find her a new home.'

Glime's beard shifted and moved in a way that Der supposed meant he was smiling. 'Welcome to Fringetown, the last known civilised place from… well everywhere,' he said.

'Nice to meet you, Glime,' Der said.

'Nice to meet you too, Der,' he said with another hidden smile.

The first signs of the morning sun shot across the endless flats, like a surging golden tide. Glime beckoned them to follow him, just as the orange waters hit the turret. Inside the turret were a series of makeshift lifts, similar to the kind used in mines. They were rickety and creaked with every slightest breeze.

Glime stepped inside the one that was closest to the door. It instantly bounced and wobbled around. Silvaran and his crew boldly stepped in, the old wooden timbers creaking under the strain. Der peered inside the lift contraption, suspiciously eyeing the crumbling timbers and rusty strapping. Her right eyebrow raised in sheer shock that the five grown men had idly stepped into what she could only describe as a death trap.

'Glime, is it safe?' she tentatively asked.

'Ah it depends how you define safe, lass,' he bellowed out, followed by a chorus of deep laughs. Der stood with her eyebrow glued to her forehead, and her hands firmly on her hips, staring at the five of them, till one by one, the seasoned pirates shifted their look and stopped laughing. Moments later there was an awkward silence.

'Look, Der, it is the only way down from The Fringeland Flats, and they don't often crash! Though we don't often have visitors!' Glime said. Der closed her eyes, stepped forward onto the lift, paused, and slowly opened her eyes, half expecting them all to be hurtling down an endless shaft surrounded by shards of the lift.

'OK! Hold on, Der,' Glime said.

Der looked around for a door to close behind them. Realising that a lift door was just wishful thinking, she grasped an old steel railing with both hands and braced herself.

There was a reluctant groaning and creaking of cogs

as Glime pulled a lever, followed by an almost weightless freefall. Der tensed in shock and horror. Looking around at Silvaran and his crew she noticed that their faces looked blissful and the picture of calm!!

The lift hurtled down for almost a full minute, before Glime gripped a large lever with both hands and using his full body weight, swung on the lever. Billows of smoke and an ear-piercing shriek filled the air. The lift lurched, bumped, and finally came to a halt, close to the entrance of a wide hand-cut tunnel.

The tunnel got busier and louder the further they went, and soon Der found herself in a bustling underground street which stretched far off into the distance, straight and vast.

At every ten paces there were entrances to side caverns which seemed to be shops of some sort, each decorated in different ways with crudely drawn signs. Some had hooks that had been pushed into the walls, for wares to be displayed on, others had makeshift tables outside in the entrance, made from rickety pieces of board, loaded with various goods.

Der glanced at the nearest one. An old woman sat on a wooden crate, her hair a silver grey and a soft smile on her face, that shifted and further carved her smile lines. She was dressed in an orange-brown garment, that resembled the colour of rust. She greeted every passer-by with her warm-hearted smile and gestured to her table which had an assortment of makeshift drinking cups. A large vat of steaming liquid was placed on her right.

One of the passers-by caught her eye contact and smiled back. With a gentle nod of the head, he handed her something and she poured an old tin cup full of the steaming liquid. The man stood chatting to the lady while sipping it.

Der let her eyes wander to the next shop, just across the tunnel. A young man stood there, his hair dusty brown, his eyes bright and alert. He leant against the doorway to the cavern and bellowed out, 'Belts! Best in town! Could save your life!'

He too was dressed in a rusty coloured garment, like most, but around his waist was a magnificent belt, holding everything from a makeshift drinking cup to a rustic knife. The belt was thick and wide, and seemed to be made of a black substance, with a scale-like texture.

'Belts! Best in Fringetown!' he called again as a new group of prospective customers wandered past. To his left was a long table that had a vast range of belts; some were thin, others were chunky and looked like they were made for endless adventures. But they were all made from the same strange black textured material.

Enticed and intrigued, Der let her eyes wander further up. Several doors down, she noticed a short old man sitting up high on a rickety collection of objects, all balanced on each other. He was craning over another man, a sharp blade contraption in his hands, cutting and styling the other man's hair, while along the wall there were several people all sitting in a queue waiting their turn for a trim.

As Der looked more closely at the walls of the tunnel, there was something else that intrigued her. There were bright colours, mixed with greys and browns and oranges. She realised that the entire tunnel was made of a mixture of metal, plastic and wooden items, all tightly compressed together to make a strange conglomerate. As she inspected closer, she could just make out recognisable items, like screws, wires, packaging and pieces of wood. The walls were like an odd rainbow.

Excited, Der wanted to browse all of the stalls and shops. But just then Silvaran tapped her on the shoulder. 'Got to keep up with Glime; you could get lost here. We're off to see Pertwin.'

Der smiled and increased her pace, keeping up with Glime, as they picked their way through the hustle and bustle of the street. After quite a long walk they came to a small shop that sold an assortment of oddly shaped items.

Sitting behind the table was a lady in her fifties, with milky eyes, unkempt hair and a kind face. She battled with her unruly hair, constantly flicking it out of her eyes, just for it to fall back in them again moments later. She too, like most of the people in the strange underground town, wore a rusty coloured garment.

She greeted Glime with a hug, then she noticed Silvaran. Her whole face lit up when their eyes met and the two rushed into a long embrace.

'Pertwin, so lovely to see you! Arc is on her way, she

is just readying the ship,' Silvaran said in a tone that sounded the softest Der had ever heard him speak.

'It's been many moons since you were down this way. What have you been up to? Have you decided to finally settle down?' Pertwin asked with a cheeky almost childlike smile.

'Settle down! Ha ha ha!' Silvaran boomed out in a hearty voice. 'There is more chance of the forests returning!'

Pertwin laughed too. 'Ah, pardon me, I've been rude. I've not offered you all buzzer cookies.' She smiled and passed out handfuls of rich brown cookies. When she noticed Der, she immediately asked, 'Who is this that's travelling with you?'

Silvaran stepped forward and explained, 'She was found alone wandering in the Last Forest. I promised to find her a safe place to live with a family.'

Pertwin moved forward to look at Der. 'Who are your family, deary?' she asked in a kind voice.

Der cast her gaze down towards the floor for a moment, in sadness. 'I don't remember anything before arriving in the forest. No matter how hard I try.'

Pertwin put her arm around Der. 'Don't worry, Der. It must be hard to not have family. You can stay with us. Skoots will show you around and you can bunk in the room next to him. You will have to muck in though,' she said in a soft and gentle voice.

Der was overwhelmed by Pertwin's kindness. 'Really? Are you sure?' she asked, taken back.

'Of course! Any friend of Silvaran's is a friend of mine. And Skoots will be overjoyed to have someone to hang out with. He will be along in a while. He can show you round while Silvaran and I discuss all the details,' she said reassuringly. Der hugged Pertwin.

'Here he is now!' Pertwin exclaimed, pointing towards a rather dusty, grimy looking boy who was riding some kind of odd contraption. It had a large wheel at the back, a small wheel at the front, a long board between the two wheels and a rusty piece of pipe attached to the front wheel forks, to which a 'T' handle had been fixed at chest level.

The boy stood on the board with one foot and kicked at the floor with his other, propelling himself forward. He wove and slid expertly around the people bustling in the street, swerving and dodging the constantly shifting obstacles in his path.

When he came close to Pertwin's stall, he spotted Silvaran and his motley crew. He narrowed his eyes and kicked harder, propelling himself on what looked like a collision course with the seasoned pirate.

Silvaran stood like an unmovable mountain, his eyes unblinking, the tiniest of smiles in the corner of his mouth as the boy-shaped blur whizzed on towards him, Der half closed her eyes in anticipation of the collision, when all of a sudden the boy's foot stopped kicking.

Der noticed that his kicking foot was wrapped in a thick piece of the same black textured material that the strange belts had been made from. In a blink, he had rotated his foot, jammed his armoured foot onto the back tyre and at the same time, flicked round the handles to the left. There was a cloud of smoke and the boy slid the back end of the vehicle around, bringing it to a halt inches from Silvaran.

Silvaran laughed, reached forward and ruffled Skoots' hair. 'I see you are still riding that thing of yours. You have grown since I last saw you!' Silvaran boomed. Skoots gave a great grin and hugged Silvaran.

'Can I join your crew yet?' the boy asked. Silvaran smiled, uncharacteristically.

'One day, Skoots, one day!' The two appeared to have a warm bond and chuckled away for a while in banter, till there was a swift interruption from a rather flustered Arc who had just arrived.

'Ship all secured and prepped, Cap. I made my way down as quickly as I could,' she said, standing tall, dressed in a fine waistcoat.

Silvaran turned to her and smiled. 'Well done, Arc, you will make an excellent captain one day,' he said, glancing at Pertwin.

Arc turned to see Pertwin staring at her with shining eyes. 'Arc, my dear, you have grown!' she just about managed to say, before Arc dashed over and gave her a long hug.

'And how is that strange little brother of mine?' Arc said, turning to look at Skoots. 'See you are still riding that death-trap, wanting to be a pirate!'

Skoots went a little red and sighed at the presence of

his big sister. 'Thought you might have been eaten by snakes by now, leaving an opening for me!' Skoots said half grinning.

'Sorry to disappoint you, baby bro. You stick to your strange "Oldie" and let me do the pirating!' she said with so much swagger, even Silvaran raised an eyebrow.

'I will make a better desert pirate than you, sis!' he said taking a step towards her. She also stepped forward, then tapped her sword hilt with her fingers.

'Want to put that to the test, little one?' she said with one of her cold hard stares.

'Hmmm,' Silvaran said, to diffuse the two. 'Stand down the both of you!' The two smiled and hugged, then turned to Silvaran. 'I would love to stop for a few days, but Arc here spotted a ship owned by a particularly nasty group called the Cockroaches. The ship was driven entirely by poor Foresters. Pertwin and I must speak a little, the crew must resupply and then we must leave at first dusk to hunt the ship down and free those slaves. Arc, I would not judge you if you wanted to sit this one out. It will be a dangerous mission.'

Arc looked a little hurt at the very idea, but stood tall, looking Silvaran square in the eye. 'I will ride with you, wherever you go, Cap,' she boomed. 'I'm not afraid of a few Roaches.'

As much as both Pertwin and Silvaran wanted her to sit it out, they knew there was no chance of stopping her.

'Silvaran, look after her please,' Pertwin said with tears

in her eyes.

'You know I will protect her with my life, dear Pertwin,' he replied in an unusually soft and tender tone, as his eyes met hers and they hugged. Then Pertwin turned to Skoots and introduced Der, suggested that he show her around while the adults discussed some business.

Skoots hugged his sister and whispered almost undetectably, 'Come back safe, sis.' Then he hugged Silvaran and turned back to Der, bursting with excitement at the idea of her staying.

The boy smiled a cheeky smile. He had milky eyes like his mother, unruly brown hair, a freckly face, round podgy nose and was covered from head to toe in grime. Round his waist he was wearing an over-large belt that was covered in strange objects. Der could not help but stare at the odd items, trying to work out what they were for.

He held up a thumb and pointed over his shoulder towards his wheeled contraption. 'Hop on, I will show you round our end of town!'

'Hey, Skoots, ride slowly with Der!' Pertwin said.

'YES, MUM!' Skoots said in mocking attitude. And before she could reply to him, Skoots had jumped on to his contraption and Der was balanced on the board behind.

The wheeled item moved with surprising smoothness and agility for what looked like a bunch of scavenged objects put together. Der gripped his shoulders tightly as they swerved round the pedestrians, some of whom seemed to know Skoots and shouted greetings to him as they passed.

Der watched the shops flash by, till after a while, they thinned out and became simple caverns with front doors. Each door was made of a mixture of materials, mostly ancient wooden boards and sheets of rusty metal. Some had makeshift windows cut into them, to make them feel more homely.

Der caught a glimpse of a few of the insides of them as people entered or exited and closed the doors behind them. They appeared to be small homes – the walls inside were the same as the street, a strange mixture of ancient, discarded items, compacted into a rock-like material.

She noticed also that the caverns had not been built with the material, but that they had been carved and hewn out of it. Each one was unique in the refashioned, cobbled together furnishings inside. The further they went down the seemingly never-ending street, the newer the cavern homes looked, till they reached some that were just empty hewn spaces. Only a few were inhabited and the doors were just rugged curtains.

Skoots gently eased his foot onto the back wheel and slowed them to a smooth stop outside the only one that had a door. He reached down into a pouch on his huge belt and produced an old key, which he held up in front of Der, then twizzled round and jiggled the key in a rusty lock.

The door creaked open to reveal a warm glowing lamp that was crudely wired up. It flickered and as Der followed him in, it went off. Skoots took an object from his waist and hit the lamp and it reluctantly went back on again.

The entrance opened out into a small round lounge. Just off from that was what looked like a tiny kitchen. An old sink was balanced on blocks of wood and metal. On the opposite side of the lounge were three more very tiny rooms. Each one, like everything else, was hewn from the strange material.

'This is my room,' Skoots said, pointing over his shoulder with his thumb. It was stocked from floor to ceiling with objects. There were wheels, cables, lengths of wood and metal. And on a makeshift desk there were a few ancient, dishevelled books and magazines.

On the wall was a large sheet of old metal. Most of the paint on the metal was still there and several diagrams were drawn. In the middle of the stacks and stacks of objects was a small bed roll, made from that same rusty coloured fabric and stuffed with something soft.

'Wow, are you an archaeologist?' Der asked, remembering Golderwin and his enthusiasm for collecting and cataloguing ancient objects.

Skoots chuckled. 'No, I like to make things.'

Der glanced back towards the door. 'Did you make that thing we rode on?'

'Yes, I did. It's called a scooter, look,' Skoots said. He

promptly clambered over some of the objects strewn on the floor and very gently picked up one of the torn old magazines. His fingers turned the pages, treating the ancient pages like a museum curator might, till he reached the middle and placed it down on the floor.

Der squinted at the very faded illustration of a new scooter. It looked like a form of transport made for people to get around in ancient times. She glanced back at Skoots' scooter, made of an assortment of cobbled items and compared it with the manufactured glossy advert in the magazine. Though his was made of a jumble of found stuff, the design certainly resembled it.

'Wow, that's nice!' Der said.

'No, it's "cool",' Skoots replied.

'Cool? It stops you getting too hot?' Der enquired.

'No! Cool is a way to say it's great; look.' He pointed to a faded picture of a kid standing next to the scooter with a speech bubble that read: 'This baby is cool'.

'Baby? Where? I don't understand,' Der said, scrunching up her face in total confusion.

'Don't worry, girl, it's just the way they used to speak years ago. The baby referred to the scooter. And cool was a word for something that was highly respected.'

Skoots pointed to another page in the magazine where there was a faded image of two kids hitting each other's hands together.

'Give me five,' he said, holding up the palm of his hand. Der held up her palm to mimic him. He extended his hand and gently slapped his palm together with hers.

Der looked perplexed at the greeting.

'Is that how you all greet in Fringetown?' she asked.

'No, Der. Just me. I love reading about the olden days and trying out the strange old phrases,' Skoots explained.

'That is…' Der paused, to try out the oddly familiar word in her mind. 'Cool,' she said tentatively.

A large smile filled Skoots' face. 'Yer, sis, you wiv that ling,' he said.

Der looked perplexed. 'Sis. Wiv… the?' she tried to repeat.

'Sorry, too much oldie. I mean, you've got it. Nice use of "cool". I hardly ever get a chance to use oldie. Most people just look at me like I am crazy,' Skoots said glumly.

'Hmm can't think why,' Der replied with a grin and punched him on the arm affectionately. They both giggled and looked through some of his books, testing out some of the "oldie speak" and spoke about some of the odd things in the pictures which were strangely familiar to Der.

'Right, Der, let's get you settled into your room. I'm afraid it was Arc's and is now the spare room and has a load of my stuff in it, so we will have to clear it out,' he explained.

'OK, sis!' Der said trying out the word.

'No, you can't do that, Der. Sis is short for sister. But I'm a boy!'

Der thought for a moment. 'OK, brother?'

'Yer, sis, you are getting it. But they didn't say

'brother' they shortened it to 'bruv',' Skoots corrected.

'Oh, OK, bruv. That's cool,' Der said with a triumphant smile.

'That's it, Der, wow you are a natural, it took me ages to use my first oldie!' Skoots said with a smile. 'Right, let's clear you a room,' he added and the two jumped up.

Der followed Skoots into the next room, where she was amused to find an even bigger pile of objects than in his room. They got to work shifting and moving the items, stacking most of it up in his room, with the remainder in the corner of the lounge. Skoots disappeared, only to reappear moments later with a fresh bed roll which he carefully arranged for her on the floor.

'Tomorrow I will show you the forage pits!' Skoots said in an excited voice. 'You will love them. Now get some sleep.'

'The forage pits. What are they?' Der asked with an excited face.

'You'll have to wait and see!' Skoots replied as he strolled out. When he got to the doorway of her room, he turned. 'Oh and, Der, welcome to your new home.' He smiled and left.

Der lay down on the bed roll. It was surprisingly soft and comfortable. She could hear faint strange sounds coming from Skoots' room next door, of things being moved around, metal being hammered and things being cut. It wasn't loud though, and soon Der was relaxing, gazing up at the dimly lighted ceiling of the small cavern she was in.

She let her eyes explore the ancient items and shapes that were in the ceiling. She got lost in the shapes, wondering what each one once was, what it was used for and who by. Before long she drifted off into a calm sleep, contented and comfortable after her long and dangerous journey. She had one of those strange dreams again, of cars and buses and hustling, bustling streets, alien, yet familiar.

As she slept, and the sunset fizzled out, the *Dawn Eagle* was being freshly repaired for its perilous mission. There was a flurry of activity as several people from Fringetown dashed around, passing materials and supplies to the crew. When the last item was loaded, Silvaran stood eye to eye with his brother Glime.

'Are you sure you want to do this, brother?' Glime asked, raising a bushy eyebrow. 'We could try to raise a few ships to help, you don't need to take them on alone.'

'Yes, Glime, I need to do this. I need to free those slaves. I wouldn't want any other ships with me, as the mission will be very dangerous, not to mention we could be scoping out Roach turf for weeks till we find their hideout. No, this is a lone mission. Would you do me a favour, Glime?' Silvaran asked, a stern and serious look in his eye.

'Yes, brother, anything, you name it,' Glime said.

'I want you to keep an eye on Pertwin, Skoots and Der for me. And if I don't make it back, you know what to do.'

Glime looked shocked at the prospect and grabbed his brother's arm. 'Now you listen here, we won't be having such talk. *When* you get back, I will welcome you with a meal, you will regale us with the story and Pertwin will expect that you stay for a week. Besides, you have to look after Arc there.'

They nodded to each other in an understanding shared by only brothers and then turned away without looking back. With that, the black sails went up and the *Dawn Eagle* sped out across the flats.

CHAPTER FOURTEEN

Der awoke on what she thought was the next evening, to the same dim lamplight that strained to reach every corner of her room. She lay still for a while, letting her mind wander back to the wild and dangerous events of the last few weeks getting to Fringetown. It had been arduous, but full of adventure.

As her mind slowly caught up, she thought of the kind lady, Pertwin, who had offered to give her a home. And Skoots, with his odd 'scooter'. She was safe and had a new family now. But still she felt frustrated that she could not remember a single concrete detail about her life before the forest.

Should she really just move on? Or were there two parents out there looking for her? It was no use. Der knew that the more she dwelled on those thoughts the worse she would feel. She had to move on, at least for now anyway.

A loud 'huhum' came from the other side of the curtain. Der sat up in her bed roll and looked at the curtained doorway.

'Yo, sis, brought you some grub!' came a familiar

voice.

Der snapped out of her daydream. 'Yer, bruv, whatever "grub" is.'

Skoots bundled through the curtains with a rusty piece of metal with something hot on it, the steam twisting and turning through the air as he approached.

'Grub is old speak for food!' Skoots explained.

'In which case grub would be cool, bruv,' Der said, trying to use as many oldie phrases as she could remember from the day before. She tucked into the makeshift bowl of hot sweet soup. It tasted familiar; similar to all the other food she had eaten since she had left the forest.

'Mmm that is nice, what is it?' she asked.

'Ah, it's beetle larva and roach soup. My mum's own recipe, with just a hint of spice from the bottle garden.' Der tried not to think of the insects while she ate it but had to admit it was delicious!

'Right, Der, we have a busy day ahead of us. Finish your grub and meet me out front in a mo!'

Der furrowed her brow. 'Mo?' she said with one eyebrow raised.

'Yer, it is short for moment.'

Der put her hands on her hips and said, 'I can't keep up with all of this oldie! At this rate I'll need a dictionary before it's even lunchtime!' They both giggled.

'Hang on a mo. Isn't grub also the name for a baby insect?' Der said with a smile.

'Er, yes, I suppose it is,' agreed Skoots.

'So, you brought me some grub… grub!' Der said with a giggle. They both chuckled at the joke, realising that they were probably the only two people in the whole world who would find it funny.

Ten minutes later, Der was ready for her first day in Fringetown. As she stepped outside the front door of the tiny cave house, she noticed Skoots standing next to two scooters.

'Sorry if I was a bit loud while you slept, I wanted to finish my spare scooter, so you could use it.'

Der looked down at the newly finished scooter. It had a large wheel on the front, a tiny one on the back and long handlebars. She inspected it all round; it was every bit as well made as Skoots' one.

'Let's ride, sis!' Skoots said as he jumped on his scooter in a flash and took off. Der was left behind, trying to work out how to balance on the contraption. When Skoots peeked back, expecting Der to be right behind him, he hit the brakes hard, slid round and sped back.

'OK, Der, let me show you the basics.'

He showed her how to balance, kick and manoeuvre. A while later and Der was scooting like a natural, almost as if she had used one before! The two sped through the street, meandering around the slowly waking population of Fringetown. They rode past empty half-dug caverns for what felt like ages, till Skoots suddenly slid to a stop at a fork in the road. Der squinted down the right-hand path.

There were people bustling around, some pushing makeshift carts and others with dull torches attached to their heads. A rough and grimy man stood at the entrance to the road. In one hand he held a large sturdy lump of wood, and in the other a dull lamp. His eyes flicked suspiciously towards everyone who passed. A man just ahead of Der and Skoots timidly walked up to him.

'Can I see your permit?' he said in a deep voice.

'Well, I, um, left it at home, gov,' the thin visitor said.

'No permit, no entrance, you know the rules. Sorry.'

'But I-I,' the wiry man tried to reason.

The guard brought his long piece of wood down onto the ground with a large bash, causing the visitor to flinch, turnabout and sharply walk off. Der hung back but could already see Skoots boldly stroll up to the guard.

'Morning, Tusket!' Skoots said in a jolly voice. The guard, much to Der's surprise, pulled his flat cap down in respect, and from his grimy worn face a big smile emerged. He patted Skoots on the shoulder.

'S'poze you want to have a forage, Skoots?' he asked.

'Love to!' Skoots replied.

'No worries; just age about ten years and go and get a permit!' the guard said with a great mocking grin.

Skoots walked back to Der. 'I was hoping old Dozer was on duty today, he is easier to slip by than a sleeping gran. But Tusket! He has the eyes of a hawk and the temper of bear,' Skoots said glumly.

'What is up there anyway?' Der said.

'That, lil sis, is the forage pits!' Skoots whispered. 'The coolest place in Fringetown. But don't worry, it has more holes than Swiss cheese!'

'Swiss cheese?' Der mumbled, about to ask, but realising that if she stopped to ask every time Skoots threw in oldie speak, the day could get very long. So she simply smiled and whispered, 'How do we get in?'

Tusket had looked away to deal with the same thin man from earlier who had come back with his permit.

'Go,' Skoots whispered, without wasting a moment.

The two of them scooted off down the left-hand path, while Tusket was preoccupied. Before long they came to several forks; each time she followed Skoots as he swerved and slid around the bends and corners. This area looked deserted, mostly a warren of narrow tunnels with very little light, completely different to the wide main street that most of Fringetown was built along.

Skoots took out a small transparent bottle and shook it. The contents writhed around and started to glow, giving off an odd green shimmer that was enough to light their way.

'What's that?' Der asked.

'Ah, these are an insect that live deep in our tunnels. They are horrid to eat, but handy as a portable lamp! All you have to do is feed them once in a while and the colony will last for years,' Skoots explained.

They moved through the tunnels slowly. Some were

impassable, due to being used as storage spaces and others were odder places still. Der only caught glimpses of them in the green glow. Noticing her curiosity, Skoots led her into one of the rooms.

It was almost completely dark and had a huge step just inside the entrance that dropped away to a large bowl-shaped floor. In the soft green glow, Der could make out thousands of dots scurrying off.

'This area is the farm; it's where we grow the insects, bacteria and fungi that we eat, make clothing from, colour things with, and even write with. The workers that tend to them only work in the night and are resting now. Let's keep moving!' he said, beckoning Der to follow.

They passed many other caverns and a few more forks, till Skoots led them into a small space that appeared to be empty and completely abandoned. He moved an old sheet of metal to reveal a hand-cut tiny tunnel, just big enough to crawl along. They stashed their scooters and crawled through the tunnel, taking care to not cut themselves on the sharp protrusions in the walls.

They came out in the secluded corner of a much larger cavern, hewn out like all the rest. There was a hive of activity, as people were hammering, cutting and chiselling out items from the walls. They slipped unnoticed along the back wall and through several tunnels, before arriving in an open space.

'They finished excavating this cavern a long time ago!

Welcome to the forage pits,' Skoots said with a large grin. He took out a makeshift hammer and chisel and began to chip away at the wall, the people in the main pit oblivious to them. Small objects fell onto the floor in a pile at his feet.

After a while of chiselling, he bent down and sifted through the pile. As he dusted away the dirt and dust that made up some of the conglomerate, Der's eyes widened to see an odd mixture of objects. There was part of a spoon, an old battery, some cabling, bolts, screws, bottle caps, plastic wrapping and some fragments of wood. He put the items in his pocket and moved to a different section of wall.

'Right, you take these and have a go for yourself!' he said to Der, handing her the hammer and chisel.

She wandered around the perimeter of the old, abandoned pit, casting her eyes over the marks left by the miners when they had torn away the main bulk of the material. She ran her fingers over the surface, wondering where to start, till she came to a tiny splash of plastic that stuck out. It was the corner of something, so she decided to excavate it with the tools. As she worked around it, she found that the protruding piece eventually connected to another much larger item, which she worked hard at, chiselling here and there in all the dips and nooks. Eventually with a rather large 'clonk' the object fell to the floor.

Skoots looked round with a jump and came rushing over. He cleaned it off and smiled. 'Do you know what this is, Der?'

'I'm not sure, but I feel it might be for... music?' Der said, following her hunch.

'Yep, sis, you just found yourself a "cassette boogie box". They were used to play music in olden times. But more importantly a great pile of salvageable saleables!'

He took out a small fabric roll that was in his pocket and unrolled it to reveal an array of handmade and scavenged tools. Selecting a long cross-head screwdriver, he carefully dismantled the machine. Once inside, he pulled out the speaker, lights, wires and motor and then tossed the rest of it to one side.

'Why are you only taking those bits?'

'There are techies and pirates that can cleverly use these parts to make things,' Skoots explained.

'But the rest of it?' Der asked, gesturing to the circuit boards and other components.

'No good to anyone. That's oldie tech far too complex for people nowadays!' Skoots said with a small scoff.

As he turned to go back to his scavenging, Der slipped the circuit board in her pocket. She was not sure why she wanted to keep it. Maybe it was the silver lines that looked like the roads from her dreams, the tiny, coloured parts, or just an absurd idea that she might tinker with it later on. She carried on chipping away at the same place, exploring the areas that had now become exposed by the void left by the boogie box.

CHAPTER FIFTEEN

A glimmer of moonlight broke through the thin clouds, making its slow and lethargic way down through the forest canopy and lighting a tightly formed circle of Virdarians, locked in a fierce, heated song. But as I imagine you are not well enough versed in Virdarian song yet, I will translate it to plain English for you.

Gladerwin was small by Virdarian standards, a clear foot shorter than the average nine feet. But what he lacked in height, he certainly made up for in years. His long grey beard flowed in an unruly manner down past his shoulders; the wrinkles of his face told of many a decade tending to the forest. He and his wife were the village elders.

He stepped forward with a red face and shook his twisted knobbly stick in the air. 'We must fight, I tell you!' he roared. 'The Aridians are now taking so much of the forest each week, that we must fight, just like our ancestors did! It is due to their formidable tenacity that we still have a forest today. It is the only thing that will stop the desert pirates. The only thing that they understand!'

'Now, now, Gladerwin dear, don't get all fired up, you know it doesn't do you any good,' his wife Brookorwin said in a soft and gentle voice. 'You know that violence does not solve everything!' she added. But it was already too late. Gladerwin's words had fired up the hearts of most of the crowd.

There was a mutter that soon turned into a roaring chant. 'FIGHT FOR THE LAST FOREST!' The sound escalated till it was a great rumbling song.

'SILENCE!' a booming voice cut through, as the second in command, Golderwin, stepped forward to speak. 'You know that I love this forest no less than the next, and I would happily protect it, if we have to. But has it really come to this? Is there no other way to stop these pirates?'

At first his words seemed to change the hearts of the group, but then two other Virdarians stepped forward in reply. 'Look, we have tried talking and reasoning with the pirates, and where has it got us? Bark here got his leg sliced badly!'

'And I got sliced on the arm.' Several more joined in. 'And I lost an ear.' 'And my wife here almost died from her wounds.'

Gladerwin's stern voice cut back in. 'No, I am sorry. We have tried listening to you, Golderwin. We have tried your diplomacy and it has cost us far too much. And all the time we are losing at least fifty trees a night. Half the time they don't even take the trees now; they just leave them burnt. No, it is time to use force to stop them.

Time to fight!' Gladerwin's face had taken on a new level of red, as he bellowed this out.

His wife tried to hush him, telling him to sit still, but it was no use, and the chant went up again. 'FIGHT FOR THE LAST FOREST!'

And at that, most of them there took up crude weapons, lengths of wood, or anything to hand and began to march in a line, in a manner never seen since that of the Great Forest War. They strode as one unit towards the forest edge, which sadly was already a great deal closer to their village in the centre than when Der had stayed there.

So much of the forest had been cut and ripped down since then, that in fact the journey to the edge of the forest took only fifty minutes. And they had calculated that if they could not stop the pirates, the forest would be gone in weeks.

Fire blazed in the Virdarians' eyes. They were at heart a peaceful people. Golderwin and many of the others had tried to stop the all-out fighting, in favour of diplomacy and softer tactics like sleepy dust.

But with every tree that fell, the fear of the Last Forest disappearing forever had increased. And little by little the population had decided to turn to violence. When they arrived at the edge of the forest, they could already see the tell-tale signs of tree felling so they decided to lie in wait for the next pirates.

***

Not too far away from the forest under a solemn cloudy sky, four great ships had stopped. They were fully laden with logs and slaves, yet not a peep came from them. The shadows danced around the desert floor as the clouds flowed across the sky, deflecting the moonbeams that illuminated four figures standing in a circle, their milky white eyes bright against their shadowed faces.

'It seems our little plan is playing off, my friends!' said the tall woman, the moonlight shimmering on the delicate curves of her pearl-white face. 'The extra logging and burning has worked a treat,' she said with a nasty candy-cane smile.

'Yes, Satisa, it has. And leaving ambushers in the forest to help the violence along when the two sides met was a fine idea, even if I don't mind saying so myself,' a short balding man with a twitching eye said as he rubbed his hands together.

'Yeah, and every time, neither the Foresters nor the other Wastelanders noticed it was us that drew the first blood; they just assumed it was each other and followed suit. That was a fine idea, Trode,' said Dorlan, straightening his cap.

'It was especially fun tonight giving those Foresters a beating, on behalf of our… fellow desert friends,' bellowed the fourth voice, larger than life and filled with sarcasm. The great bulky woman was swinging her massive club up and down, thumping it onto her other hand in a menacing way.

'Glad we asked you along, Growser!' Dorlan said with

a grin. 'My spies tell me that they are so angry, they are marching to the edges of the forest, looking for a fight.'

'Excellent work, my friends,' said Satisa with a silky smooth smile. 'It's only a matter of time until both sides go to war. Let's chop even more trees and make sure that when both sides find each other, they fight at every single opportunity.'

A dark wall of cloud slid back over the moon, returning the four faces into shade, as Satisa said, 'Oh, and associates, watch out for the Fulgur tonight. It loves to strike when the moon is veiled.'

The others looked up at the eerie sky and unusual clouds and shuddered at the thought of the beast. Glancing at each other sheepishly to ensure they were not showing any sign of fear, they scuttled back to the ships. The flags went up and the ships set off at double time.

***

Well into the night, two young figures sat deep in discussion, poring over a handmade book.

'Hey, bro, let's add those new words we found in your friend's book to our oldie speak collection. What was it again? Twenty-three skidoo?' Der reached for an old biro that was brown from age, but still had a few dregs of ink left.

Skoots handed her the raggedy book on a new page and she jotted it down. 'Yes way, sis! Oh, and don't forget to not be a square and to not flip your lid!' he said with a chuckle.

'Oh, ain't that a bite,' Der said as she tried to tease the last of the ink out of the biro to complete the 'L' in lid. She rummaged around in her pocket to see if she had another, pulling out an assortment of items. There were a few small tools she had collected over the past few visits to the forage pits, an old piece of circuitry, a speaker and a tiny solar panel from a calculator.

'Why do you keep all that old tech, Der? I told you before it's far too complex for anyone to do anything with. You have a ton of it in your room.'

Der looked slightly embarrassed. 'Oh, you know, I guess I just like it!' Der explained. She glanced down at the speaker and components, then stretched up her arms, giving a giant yawn.

'Boy I am pooped! I think I'm going to hit the sack!' she said, gently scooping up the contents of her pocket and making her way to the door.

'Night, Der!' Skoots said. 'Night my BFAM!'

Der settled into bed and waited patiently for the cavern to fall silent and everyone to sleep. As little by little it fell silent, she grew more excited. It was her favourite time of the day. She had a great deal of fun in the daytime with Skoots, getting in and out of mischief, and she dearly loved her new life. But at night, when everyone was asleep, it was her absolute favourite.

She slipped out of bed and gave a couple of bottles a shake, instantly letting off that all familiar green glow. Skoots was right, she really had collected a lot of electronics. But what he didn't know was what she did with them!

She pulled a collection of parts out of an old box that she kept hidden in the corner and placed each component out in order on the floor, first the boogie box circuit board, then some wires and an odd collection of other items. She pulled out roll of tools that she had made with the help of Skoots and began working.

She had no idea how she knew what to do, but she did. Her fingers had a mind of their own as they twisted wires together and she had soon created some kind of electronic device. She placed the circuitry into a rugged wooden box, lined the lid with solar panels and wired them in, then double-checked everything.

'Hmm, yes, I think it might just work,' she whispered and slipped the box safely beside her bed. She crawled under her covers, closed her eyes and fell asleep.

A familiar voice pulled Der out of a deep dreamless sleep. 'Oy, wake up, sleepy head, and get into your foraging threads!'

She opened her eyes and glanced around the room, after what had felt like only a few minutes' sleep. A great cheeky grin hovered over her.

'Come on, don't be a square!' the grin chuckled.

The events of the night began to filter slowly back into Der's head and she glanced over at the box. A smile slipped over her face as she realised that it was not just a dream.

'Listen, Skoots, I have something to show you!' she

said in an unusually serious tone.

'Well, spill the beans!' he replied, curiosity getting the better of him.

'If I show you this, promise not to laugh if it doesn't work and to keep it secret!' she said with a concerned look.

'I'm your BFF, I'm your ride or die! We are fam! Of course!' he confirmed.

Der held out the box for Skoots to see.

'Err, what is that?' he asked, perplexed.

Der placed it down on the floor and gently lifted the lid to reveal the circuitry that she had wired up.

'Err, I know what the solar panels do, we have large ones in the desert powering the dim lights in our town, but the rest just looks like bits of circuit,' Skoots said, trying to wrap his head around the contraption.

'We need sunlight to power it. Is there any way we can go outside?' Der asked.

'Well, not up through the main shafts, that's for sure. At this time of the day, it would take you out into the mid-morning desert and you would likely dehydrate, cook, burn or combust. Or dehydrate, cook, burn and combust all at once. People only go out there at night, to leave town, or to check the solar panels,' he explained.

'Ahhh,' Der said with a look of utter disappointment.

'Look, there might be a place though,' Skoots replied. 'It's difficult to get to, but it would give you indirect sunlight.'

'What, without the cooking and inconvenience of

combusting?' Der asked jokingly.

'Yes! But if we are to get there, we need to beat feet, and twenty-three skidoo!'

Precisely thirty seconds later, Der was standing outside the cavern, with a shoulder bag filled with provisions and her precious box. Skoots appeared moments later with a similar bag and a look of mischief.

Their long ride through the streets took them back to their usual sneak-in point, past the guards, and into the warren of tunnels. This time, though, instead of the already considerable ride to the forage pits, they kept on going, till the passage opened out again into a broad road similar in size to the main street of Fringetown. But here there were no side caverns, just one long, badly lit tunnel that seemed to go on for an eternity.

After a good many hours, Skoots slid his scooter to a stop, and suggested taking a break for some food.

The two sat down on the floor with their backs against the wall and laid out the last-minute picnic they had grabbed in a hurry. They ate in silence, so hungry after such a long scoot.

'Right, let's put the pedal to the metal,' Skoots said once they had finished. 'You're going to love this place, Der, it's a real cherry!' At once he had jumped up and scooted off.

Der ran to her scooter and took chase. It wasn't long before she had caught him up and the two were jostling each other to get ahead, sliding and skidding round corners until they turned the final corner and were met with a bright light.

They both slammed their feet on the back wheel and slid to a stop. Blinded by the intensity of the light after having spent so long down in the dim tunnels of Fringetown, they dropped to their knees, shielding their eyes.

'Reach for your shades, your solar shields, your sun cheaters, your glints,' Skoots reeled off, while frozen like a deer in headlights.

'Alright, I catch your drift! I'm looking for my sunglasses now,' Der replied.

After a moment or two of blind rummaging, they pulled out large blocky pieces of rubber in which they had set lenses scavenged from old sunglasses. They stretched the rubber strips around their faces; as they filtered out the glare and their eyes adjusted, they slowly relaxed. Getting to their feet, they leant the scooters against the wall and tentatively walked to the opening.

When they emerged, they were standing on a large rock shelf cut a little way down a cliff face. Der gasped in awe. 'It's fantabulous!' she muttered. 'Bodacious!' she continued.

She gazed up at the great gorge's mouth above them and the warm glow reflecting from the bright red cliffs. On both sides, the jagged, undulating lines of the cliff face rippled away into a haze. Der dropped slowly to the ground and wriggled over to the edge, to peer down. It was a sheer drop to what looked like a broad river flowing through the gorge far, far below.

'What is this place?' Der asked.

'Glime says the platform was built to take out the bulk of foraged goods to be sold and traded all over, including at Balldock. The goods are winched up by hand from large desert ships at night. But I like to come here in the day. The gorge protects us from the main heat and light of the desert sun.'

He suddenly looked quite excited and pointed to Der's bag. 'Well, let's see if it works, old-tech girl,' he said with a smile.

They crouched down together and Der carefully took out the box. She set it down on the brightest spot and turned on a switch. Suddenly there was a hissing noise which made Skoots jolt back a little. She slowly turned a small dial that she had wired up onto the side of the box, listening carefully to the changes in the static hiss. She wasn't sure quite why she knew how to operate the device, but it came to her by instinct.

'Are you trying to find a station?' Skoots asked with a sceptical look.

'Yes, I think I am,' she muttered without taking her gaze from the dial.

'But you won't find a station still in operation. It's old tech, no one uses it anymore!' he said, patting Der on the shoulder.

Just then, the hiss changed tone and as she slowly tuned it, it became a very faint voice. Der and Skoots looked at each other, both sets of eyebrows joining in the middle, threatening to never return to the top of their eyes. Their mouths dropped wide open as sheer surprise took over. It was two whole minutes before one of them spoke.

'Is that…' Skoots muttered, barely believing his ears.

'A radio broadcast…' Der completed in a mumble. 'I thought I could get it working, but didn't expect to find a station.'

'Yes, and do you know what this means, Der?' Skoots said excitedly, hardly pausing between words.

'I'm good at fixing things?' she said tentatively.

'No. I mean yes, you are good at fixing things. But what it actually means is that somewhere out there, there are other people. People that still use old tech. Oh that's so exciting, Der. If only there was a way to know where they were!'

Der drifted off into an odd thoughtful state, her fingers drawing patterns in the dust beside her. 'There might be a way, if we had, or could draw a map of the local area. And if we had a device to give us directions, like the one in that mag we saw last week. And finally… the most difficult part, we had some way to travel around in the desert.' She paused, realising the magnitude of the challenge.

'Oh, just that, sis? piece of cake!' Skoots said with a grin. 'You're serious?' he continued, realising Der was actually contemplating somehow locating the signal.

'Well, I do have this…' he said, pulling out a needle.

'And this.' He took out the rather battered body of an old compass. 'I was going to try to make a working one, like in that mag!' he said, with a grin that Der recognised now. It was his *I am about to get into an exciting project* grin.

'What about a map, though?' Der asked.

'I was just thinking about that. I think we should ask one of Mum's friends, Drinda. She has a shop down by the lift shafts and sells all sorts of desert pirate artefacts!'

'Schweet!' Der exclaimed, punching the air.

'It's the transport that bothers me the most,' Skoots continued. 'Sure, I could build a small desert ship, but there are so many pirates and dangers about, we would be seen and probably robbed, taken off as slaves, or eaten by snakes! Not to mention the Fulgur,' he added with a look of fear.

'How big is the Fulgur? And how long has it been around?' Der asked.

'I don't know. I occasionally hear travellers speak of it. They say it's gigantic, angry and has blue fire. And the stories seem to go as far back as our people have lived in the desert, so it must be ancient, or one of many.'

'Can it be killed or outrun?' she asked.

'Killed? No, not likely! Outrun? Well, rumour has it that a few including Silvaran have managed to outrun it at full speed.'

'Silvaran has seen it! I thought as much,' Der said.

'Yes, but he won't speak about it, not even to my mum. All we know is he lost crew that night and only got away by the speed of his ship.'

Der looked ponderous for a moment. 'So our ship would have to be small, really, really fast, and unseeable!' she said, thinking aloud. 'Like that plane we saw in your mag the other day. What was it called?'

'The stealth. Yeah, a stealth desert ship, now that would be bodacious, lit, sick, wicked, to the max, groovy!' Skoots said in a frenzy of excitement.

'Now, don't you think you're overusing those old-speak phrases? I'm pretty certain they were never designed to all go into the same sentence,' she laughed, while pondering on the word stealth.

'Do you think you could build a fast, ultra-light desert ship?' she asked with a cheeky smile.

'Probably, if I can forage enough parts!'

'So, let's do it!' Der said while standing up, with a new look of determination.

'Er, are you actually being serious?' Skoots said with a furrowed brow.

'Er, yeah. Totes!' she replied.

'Hang on, I thought we were joking around. You think we should actually try to build a compass and a stealth desert ship and find a map, then go off on an adventure to look for some radio signal?' he said in surprise.

'Yep. Let's get to work!' She picked up the box, turned and walked back to the tunnel, leaving Skoots standing there in contemplation.

'Hey, are you coming or what?' Der shouted back.

Skoots shook his head in disbelief at what he had just

agreed to. 'OK, then,' he muttered, and turned to follow.

'Last one back is a wet blanket!' Der shouted, as she kicked off on her scooter.

Soon they were jostling and panting hard, as they tried to get ahead of each other, swerving and sliding round corners and kicking till their hearts were hammering in their chests.

CHAPTER SIXTEEN

It had been many weeks since that beautiful moment on the ledge. Der and Skoots had spent every waking hour assembling the pieces for their great project.

Those faint and distant words, the thought of someone out there broadcasting still, had fired them up. They lay awake every night chatting about where and who it might be, imagining and sharing stories of a place where people were still living like oldies, using tech as the oldies did and living in comfort.

Their story had evolved each night. And every so often they would take that long and perilous journey down the tunnels back to the ledge to listen to the words, in case they had dreamt them.

Der had almost no space to sleep in her room, as it was stacked from floor to ceiling with old electronics. Even Skoots' already packed room soon became too small. It was then that they had decided to make a secret camp, far, far down the tunnels, in one of the very old disused caverns.

It had taken them days to scope one out, so far off the beaten track that no one would ever bother them.

And when they had found it, they secretly moved all their things to the cavern and began to really go to work. Skoots had told his mum they were staying at a friend's, to cover for their long absences. They would go down for days at a time, working together tirelessly to build the ultimate stealth ship.

The Lab, as they fondly referred to it, had its own light source which Der had managed to build, much to Skoots' surprise, from bulbs and solar panels with cable leading to the edge. She could also use it to test some of her designs.

Skoots found himself baffled at how Der could manipulate tech. But equally Der was always surprised by how insanely good Skoots was at engineering and making things.

The Lab was in one of the very outermost caverns, close to the ledge they had visited. They had agreed that it would allow them to winch up the ship when it was ready and launch it in secret, as long as they avoided delivery times.

The Lab was a large solitary cavern with a good sized entrance that they had covered with a makeshift door. Although it was roomy, the piles of accumulated parts made it look quite small.

Around the edges, they had set up simple work benches; at the back they had attached sheets of metal to the walls, so they could draw their designs and calculations. Strewn around the place were books and magazines that Skoots had borrowed from all over

Fringetown, from people he had helped over the years. And in the centre of the cavern was the object of so much sweat and tears.

It was a tiny vehicle, with just three bicycle wheels. The chassis was extremely low, incorporating two seats, that allowed the riders to stretch out their legs and operate pedals. Its sail was small, but very well designed, efficient enough to use ninety-nine per cent of the wind, according to Skoots.

There was also pedal power and something that Der called the DMAD, which she said was short for Dynamo Motor Assisted Drive. She explained that it would reuse the kinetic energy of the ship and transfer it back into an electric motor, to increase the speed. There was also a whole bank of solar panels, which she used to power the stealth unit.

'Hey, sis, how does this bad boy work again?' Skoots asked, pointing to the odd mass of wires and electronics that sat at the riders' eye level.

'Oh, Skoots, don't be a narbo. This is like the fiftieth time you have asked! So, you sit here and I sit here. When we're moving, the solar panels and the DMAD power this screen. It uses these units on the front, the infrared and thermal imaging cameras, to display the surroundings on the screen, so we can move through the desert without lights, navigating by the display. It's simple really. The difficult part was finding still working units and powering them,' she said with a grin.

'Sorry, narbo and noob I might be, but how do you

even know that?' he asked.

Der looked down and played with one of the patches on her trousers. 'I, I really don't know. I see things in those magazines, I seem to recognise and find things in the pits I know how to fix. But I have no idea. But it will work!' she replied with conviction.

'You're legit, sis! The bees' knees at tech. I think we're almost ready for a test run! Let's do some final checks and then get this baby up top!' he said with a grin that stretched from ear to ear.

'What did you tell Pertwin? We might be gone for a few days,' Der said with a worried look.

'Ah, don't worry about Mum, she thinks we're round at my friend Croon's place. And I gave Croon enough saleables to keep him tight-lipped and covering for us for months!' Skoots said.

'Roger that! Let's blow this taco stand!' Der said, punching her fist in the air.

'What?' Skoots said, looking like that last old-speak had left him completely baffled.

'You know, let's blow this taco stand. You know, twenty-three skidoo. Let's beat feet,' she restated.

'Ah, you're getting fly with that oldie, sis!' Skoots said. 'Right let's get this baby up top.'

An hour later they were all packed and had done a kit check at the top of the cliff. They had practised and planned the use of the cargo winch quite a few times over the last week and despite it being laden with the real ship and gear this time, their well-oiled plan had gone smoothly.

At last, they were sitting in the darkness, strapped into their seats with their supplies and gear stashed behind them ready to leave. They used a compass bearing to start the ship moving, and then when the dynamos kicked in, they switched to night vision mode.

As soon as the first breeze was in the sail, Der engaged the DMAD and the invisible ship whirred into action. It was even faster than they had imagined and they both had to focus on keeping it steered gently and on course.

All they could see in the pitch black of the night was the tiny navigation screen and the compass, but by now they knew the routes off by heart, having rehearsed each section of the journey.

It was a relatively clear and quiet night; the cold wind rushed past them as they soared across the surface of the desert, the wheels barely touching the ground. They were at reading zone one in no time at all.

Once they reached the position, they fired up the radio, tuned it to the signal of the faint voice, and took a reading of signal strength. Der momentarily used a glow lamp to write it on the map she had stashed safely in her coat before they left.

As soon as they had the reading, they set off again. With the wind in their sails and the DMAD, they were moving even faster than before, so they both had to watch the display intently.

About halfway to reading zone two, they spotted the first light of a desert pirate ship, but they circumnavigated it with ease, with no sign that they had been seen. The stealth ship worked!

They spotted another and another, and each time slipped by without arousing the slightest suspicion. Der was quietly amused at the thought of the dumb pirates, blissfully unaware that they had just been passed by two youngens in a ship that could outrun them about ten times over.

Skoots punched Der on the arm and whispered, 'Your stealth drive is on fleek! Phat, the cat's pyjamas. I really dig it.'

Der glanced at him. 'Hey homey, I'm pretty sure you can use too much oldie, you know!'

They chuckled together, then pressed on towards the next reading zone where they took the second reading, recorded it, and zoomed on. After the third and final reading zone, they sped towards the rest point.

The very first signs of morning were beginning to trickle over the horizon, when suddenly there was a clunk and the left wheel slowly started to lock up. The ship lurched to the left and they wrestled with the controls to stop it from overturning.

Skoots jumped off and looked at the wheel that had snagged up. 'Ah, no!' he exclaimed in panic.

'What's the beef?' Der asked, concerned by his tone.

'The sand has got in and bound up the bearing. If we don't switch it and make tracks, we will be sitting ducks, and this whole thing will be a nothing-burger!'

'OK, what can I do to help?' Der asked.

'Pass me the wrench and the spare wheel, asap.'

Der rushed around to the back of the ship, grabbed the bits needed and dashed back. They both set to work at switching out the wheel as quickly as they could.

Just as the rising sun began to lighten the sky in a faint twilight, they jumped back in and sped off at top speed for the rest place. Just in time, they pulled up at the entrance of a small cave that had been marked on their map. It had been a risk, whether it would be there, as the map was hand-drawn and quite old, but sure enough it was.

They pulled the ship inside and Skoots began to strip the wheels off it, cleaning and greasing the bearings, while Der pored over the readings on the map.

After a busy morning working on their separate tasks, they eventually sat down at the back of the small cave. The strong midday sun had found its way around the mouth of the cave entrance and lit up the inside with a warm golden glow.

The narrow cave-mouth opened out slightly into an irregular shaped cavern. Its walls were a dark red sandstone, and it showed signs of having been used as a rest-over spot. A blackened area in the middle marked where many a traveller had made a fire, and there was a large rock that appeared to have been used to grind herbs or grain. On the wall behind them several names had been carved.

Der and Skoots lay back half exhausted and gazed up at the odd wall of fame. They read a few to see how they sounded and wondered who they were and what they had done.

'Gen Brine. What do you think he looked like?' Der asked.

'Ah, he was a large man, with steel blue eyes and a weathered face!' Skoots said, letting his imagination run wild. 'He looked after cattle and came here to rest for the night as he moved around with his herd. And what about Smar Toak?'

'Oh old Smar,' Der mused. 'He was a travelling salesman. He wandered the old lands from town to town selling anything and everything. He was a smart and charming man, well dressed and always polite. He used this cave as a store.'

And so their imaginative banter continued. An hour passed as they lay there joking and laughing.

'I'm hungry. Let's have a spot of lunch and talk about our next move!' said Skoots, already reaching for the food pack they had taken with them. He sped off to the cave entrance and placed a handful of large beetles on a shiny piece of metal before running back. 'Now count to two-forty!'

Four minutes later he sped back to the cave entrance and returned with a smoking hot tray of grilled insects, which they tucked into, trying to silence their stomach groans, like two trapped beasts.

'I've serviced and greased the wheels and bearings, and managed to make covers to keep the dust and sand out. They should last now,' Skoots announced.

Der pulled out the map that they had recorded the three signal readings and laid it out on the soft brown dirt at their feet. They gathered around it and Der explained.

'At each of the three locations, we found the direction that the signal was strongest. I've drawn lines from each point, and where they meet is where the signal should be coming from. Right there!' she exclaimed, while pointing to a mark on the map that didn't seem to have a lot of detail drawn.

'That's another night's ride away; what should we do?' Skoots asked.

'Well, we've already travelled halfway there, and even more importantly, managed to get the stealth ship out of Fringetown without being seen. I vote we go on tonight and find the signal,' Der said with a tone of determination.

'You do have a point. OK, I agree. Let's leave first thing tonight and sail there. Can you navigate us there?' Skoots asked.

'I should be able to. Let's get some sleep and wake up just as the sun goes down.'

The orange fingers of the setting sun crept into the cave, bathing everything in warm fiery light. Skoots packed up the ship and prepared everything, then he gently shook

Der's shoulder.

'Wake up, sleepy head, it's time to go,' he said softly.

They were soon ready. The first of the diamond stars were in the velvety sky as they pulled the desert ship out of the cave and prepared to leave.

Soon they were gliding effortlessly across the Flatlands, and then between two vast rocky slopes, sailing in pitch black and absolute silence. They didn't see a single other craft, as they sailed up the narrow valley.

On and on they cruised, with just the sound of the whispering wheels, the soft sand beneath them and the wind fluttering at the sails. They gazed at the night sky as it became darker and filled with stars.

They struggled to stay awake, but kept a close watch on each other, nudging and tapping each other, when one dropped off to sleep.

They watched the two moons arc across the sky. One was large that night and they could almost make out the craters that they had seen in books. The other was far smaller and moving a lot faster, an odd grey colour, smooth and detail-less.

As the long night of solitary travelling began to take its toll on them, the track suddenly began to wind upwards. The slope was hard going, but with the help of the wind and the DMAD they finally made it to the top with the last of their energy.

The slope led to a wide ledge about halfway up the cliffside. The momentum carried them a little way along it, and some gentle pedalling took them the rest of the way. Soon the ledge sloped gently upwards again, plateauing to another flat ledge, which led to an odd shaped rock, completely different to all the others around. It was a soft grey, smoother and less irregular than the red-brown sandstone.

Skoots got out of the ship's seat and approached the strange rock. It cast a little shade, which gave them a much-needed break from the early morning sun that was already beginning to heat the area up.

They both stumbled around the side of the rock to see where it led and to their astonishment, found themselves face to face with an ancient door.

CHAPTER SEVENTEEN

The door was twice their height and looked like it had once been made of a sturdy metal, with round-topped studs that surrounded the panels. In the centre was a long metal bolt with the remains of a padlock.

Der reached forward to touch the door, but her fingers simply passed straight through, leaving two holes. As Skoots stepped towards it to investigate, there was a crunching sound, like eating crisps, and a cloud of brown dust. The remains of the door had crumbled into flaked shards of rust at their feet, and they were staring into a dark room.

'Good job it was locked,' Skoots said, without looking away.

'This isn't a rock; it's some kind of old building!' Der said. They both took one step inside, the cool air a relief after so much time in the sun, and were immediately hit with a dank, musty smell.

All they could hear was their accelerated breathing. Tentatively they stepped further into the blackness and the smell increased. The light from outside barely made it past the entrance.

Skoots felt Der reach for his hand and they held hands to muster bravery as they stood, frozen to the spot, listening, wondering. They thought they heard noises from further inside and their imaginations began to run wild. They stood for what felt like an eternity, too afraid to go any further and equally afraid to turn their backs and run.

Der slowly reached into her shoulder bag for a glow jar. As she pulled it out, the faint green glow washed over the murky interior. Suddenly there was a flicker of movement towards them. Instinctively they both dropped to the floor, before realising that they had simply disturbed some roosting bats that had found their way in. They giggled and stood back up.

Shining the timid glowing jar around, they could just make out that they were standing in a small room made from a smooth grey material, just like many a building they had seen in the oldie books. Rows of chairs were lined against one wall, made from metal tubing with curved plastic back rests, and the remains of low tables dotted between them.

Der bravely strode over to one of the seats and said, 'I'm pooped.' She promptly sat on the chair, which almost as promptly collapsed under her weight with a loud clang, the plastic backrest staying behind her as she found herself sitting in a pile on the floor.

Skoots let out a great giggle. 'Looks like the moisture has weakened them!'

He held out his hand to help her up and they stepped

a little further in. The dim light revealed a desk with a chair behind it.

'Look, a phone!' Der exclaimed in sheer delight pointing to the desk.

'Wow, and it's the real McCoy too. Look, it's still wired in,' Skoots said, exploring the long trail of cables that meandered across the desk.

'This is an archaeological site,' Der mused. 'Do you realise we're probably the first people to have been here? Should we go back to Fringetown to tell someone?'

They both looked at each other and said in synchronisation, 'NERRR.'

'Do you think it still works?' Der said, reaching down to pick it up. She gently put the receiver to her ear, imitating the images she had seen in books.

'Yes, yes. OK, sorry. Yes, I will tell him,' she said, then put the receiver down. Skoots looked horrified for a moment.

'Who was that?' he said.

'Your mum. You're in big trouble, and you're grounded for… EVER!' Der said with a gigantic guffaw.

Skoots rumbled into laughter too. As they continued to shine the dim light around, they noticed a large, heavy door close to the far corner, very different to the one they had – quite literally – walked through.

Der pushed against the door, expecting it to crumble, but it didn't. It was a little taller than the average person, and made of a shiny silver metal which still gleamed as if it had only just been made. It seemed very out of place in a room that was otherwise ancient in sight and smell. There was not a single blemish on the door, nor its heavy frame.

Skoots inspected it more closely, trying to work out how it was designed to open. After a while he pointed out the large runners that it sat on; it was designed to slide open and closed. There was no handle or way to physically open it.

Der ran her fingers around the frame, stopping about halfway up the left-hand side at something that felt different. Grabbing the glow jar from Skoots, she shone it on the area and found a small square pad that housed a button in the middle.

'Look, it opens with a button,' she declared. Extending her index finger, she grinned and pressed the button forcefully, expecting the door to open. There was nothing but a faint, tired whirring.

'It's electronic,' Der said. 'We could try to prise it open, and if that fails we should go back to Fringetown and bring equipment to try to open it. Maybe large solar panels and cables.'

'Let's see if we have anything to open it with,' Skoots said, making his way out of the building. Der reluctantly stood up too and followed him to help.

Their ship was still in a small patch of shade that the building cast. They went to work searching through the bags of equipment they had brought, looking for anything that would open the heavy door.

As Der was rummaging, a small box-like item

tumbled to the floor. It hit with a thud and broke into three parts. She knelt down and picked the pieces up carefully, like it was a broken egg.

'Oh, that was clumsy,' she muttered. She cupped the broken pieces close to her, to ensure that they didn't come apart anymore and strode off back to the cool shady building and its now dull green glow. After dusting it off, she placed the broken item on one of the low coffee tables and traced the wires that were hanging out of the broken box.

'It's OK, it's just the box that gave way. I can fix it,' she muttered to herself as she pulled her tool-roll out from her shoulder bag and began to lovingly repair the object, piece by piece. Sitting for a moment, she allowed a wave of warm memories to wash over her, of that ledge back at Fringetown where they had used this device to hear the radio signal, and their crazy dream that had sparked this whole adventure.

She slowly glanced around at the inside of the ancient grey site and then back at the box. She gave a tiny shrug, a little deflated at the fact that they hadn't found any people, or a whole lot else. She tested the buttons and dials that she had mounted on the box. Then she gently took it back outside and placed it in the sun.

'Come on, don't be broken for ever!' she said, before switching it on. There was a sound of static which changed as she twisted the dial, just like that time in Fringetown. Then the static dissipated and there was a sound. But this time it was clear.

'Look to the moon,' a voice said. There was a pause, then it repeated the same message. A simple loop, repeating over and over. Der screwed her face up in confusion.

'What's that supposed to mean?' Skoots whispered from right next to her. He had wandered over without her noticing, intrigued by what she was doing.

'Your guess is as good as mine. This feels like a… what did the oldies used to say… a wild chicken chase?'

'A wild goose chase?' Skoots pitched in.

'Ah yes, that's the one, bro!' she confirmed.

'Hang on a sec, we're asking the wrong questions! Is that signal definitely coming from this building?' Skoots asked, his hand stroking his chin in a contemplative pose.

'Yes, I'm sure of it,' Der said.

'Well, if it is, then how is it powered?'

It took a moment for the question to seep into the spongy recesses of Der's lethargic mind, then suddenly she jumped to her feet in an explosion of energy.

'You're right! Absolutely right! Skoots, you're a genius!' she exclaimed, barely pausing between words. 'There has to be some kind of self-autonomous power, in or on this building.' She rushed off before Skoots could even begin to decode what Der had said.

She ran over to the wall of the building that jutted out from the rock and shouted back, 'Are you going to just stand there, or are you going to give me a bunk up?'

Skoots ambled over. 'OK I'm here. What's a bunk

up?'

Der started to explain and then gave up. Instead, she said, 'Put your hands together, linking your fingers for me to put my foot in and help me climb up there.'

She grappled with the rough grey surface, using a combination of Skoots and footholds on the wall to clamber up onto the roof. It was made of the same grey material as the rest of the building and was not much higher than a single storey.

Once on top, Der glanced around. She could see that the roof went back a little way before it hit the surface of the rest of the cliff behind it. It was covered with dust and small stones that had accumulated over time.

She estimated that the area they had been in already was below this roof, but that the locked door must be further beyond and actually inside the cliff. She scanned around for cables or any other tell-tale signs of electronics.

She took a large step forward onto the heaps of dust and stones, when all of a sudden her foot slid. She almost went head-over-heels backwards off the roof, when she felt a hand grab her arm and steady her. She spun her head round to see Skoots standing next to her with a grin.

'You were almost game over there, sis,' he said with a hint of smugness.

Der took a moment to compose herself then peered down. It had not looked that high from the ground, but it certainly did from up there. She gulped. 'Thanks, bro,

I can be a real narbo sometimes. Just as well you were there to save my bacon!'

'Always, sis,' Skoots said, giving her a hug.

She glanced down at the roof to see what she had slipped on. There was a great slide mark in the gravel and dust, and a shiny patch of material, similar to glass.

'What?' she declared as she knelt down, dusting off more of the dirt and gravel to her right, to reveal more of the glossy material.

'There's a solar panel under all this. Help me clear it off. I bet this powered the doors and whatever is inside. Come on, Skoots. Let's clear it off and investigate what awaits behind that door.'

Skoots jumped into action immediately and they used their hands to shift the debris, scooping and throwing handfuls at a time.

Little by little they worked, enabling them to advance further onto the roof, till as the sun began to descend and the rocks started to take on the soft orange glow that announced the sun slipping over the horizon, they cleared the last of it.

'Quick, before we lose the last of the light, let's try that door,' Skoots said, scrambling down the wall unaided like a monkey. He stood at the bottom to help Der climb down, then they both rushed inside to the locked door.

Der prodded the button and immediately there was a whirring followed by a hiss, and finally the door rumbled smoothly open. They wasted no time and stepped into the dark space that was revealed.

There was a click and a series of lights flickered into action. Not grimy, dim lights or bioluminescent glow lamps, but bright, crisp lights.

They illuminated a circular room with no windows, the floor and walls made of a smooth metal. At intervals around the edge of the left-hand side of the room were curved sleek desks, made of a shiny white material.

Skoots glanced over to the nearest desk and eyed up a comfortable looking chair, that despite its age was in far better condition than the one they had found in the entrance outside. In fact, everything was. He strolled over to the desk to quench his curiosity, his footsteps reverberating loudly off the echoey walls.

On the desk were the remains of ancient paper folders, then five flat black screens lined up next to each other, each supported by a single wide foot connected to a wide base. Cabling ran in and around them, and in front of them were a couple of long slabs covered with familiar markings.

Below the desk was a large metal box with a whole spaghetti of wiring spilling out. Der clomped her way over, the loud echoes bouncing off the metallic walls.

'What…' she started to say, till she realised that the echo had increased the volume of her voice. She swallowed and tried again, in a low voice close to a whisper.

'What is all this stuff? Look at these markings, it's the language of oldie people.'

Skoots, not daring to touch anything, angled his head and contorted himself trying to look all around the different objects. But Der stood staring, as if in a trance.

The items on the desk were strangely familiar. Then something else caught their eyes. Beyond the desk was a large metal box with a translucent door. It towered above both of them and almost touched the shiny metallic ceiling. As they approached it, they were aware of a humming sound and lines of brightly coloured lights.

'What is this place?' Skoots asked.

'I really don't know. This tech is very old, yet appears to be still functioning. I think that when we cleaned off the solar panels, everything started up. And that door seems to have protected everything inside from weather, moisture and dust.'

Suddenly there was a loud beeping noise which seemed to be coming from the shiny glass box with the flashing lights. The lights blinked faster and one by one turned off, starting from the top. They stood watching, transfixed, as the last lights flickered and went out. The whirring slowly subsided, and a single larger light went on inside the box.

Without warning, the lights in the room went out, plummeting the room into darkness. Skoots and Der froze where they were, not knowing what to do.

Skoots reached for his bag and let out a sigh when he realised he had left it outside. Der had hers though and pulled out a glow lamp. The weak glow barely lit the immediate area around them.

They stayed next to each other and slowly made their way to the door. When they reached it, Der let out a sigh of relief and jabbed the button expecting it to open. But nothing happened. 'Electric is off. I guess the sun went down.'

They both slumped against the door. The darkness beyond their small green island of light stretched out like an endless ocean, and the silence began to hum in their ears.

They sat, neither of them speaking for a while. They were both trying to process the strange events that had unfolded that day: the journey across the Flatlands, through the valley, and then finding the untouched ruin. And finally getting through that door and discovering an archaeological site that was perfectly preserved.

Der's imagination began to run wild, contemplating what the place had been used for, imagining the people that had worked and possibly even lived there. She wondered what other amazing discoveries she might find in the room.

'Skoots. What do you think this place was?' she whispered.

But there was no answer – at least not the kind Der had been hoping for. Just the gentle whisper of a snore. She could just make out his features in the dim light.

She smiled. Skoots was the closest thing she had to family and was like the best friend she had never had. She was so glad they had shared so many adventures together. Her eyes fluttered as she too began to fight off the exhaustion of an almost twenty-four-hour day. And soon she too was gently snoring away.

***

Far off in the sheltering darkness of the Barren mountains, four watchful figures crouched on a rocky precipice. Far below, a heaving mass of Cockroaches danced and rioted around a fire, their faces painted red, their eyes wide and chaotic.

Some lay drunk, passed out on the floor from some numbing drink. Others were fighting over some of the spoils of a recent plunder. Some on the side-lines sprawled out eating, entertained by their fellow lawless kind.

And atop a large chair overlooking them all, sat their leader, laughing and amused by her brood as they jostled each other and fought like a pack of wild dogs. She sat contented, gorging on the best spoils, the lioness's share, fanned and waited on by slaves.

'We have finally got them,' Silvaran whispered to his crew. 'I knew it was only a matter of time before they tried to attack another ship and we could track them back to their hideout.'

'So, what's the plan, Cap?' Arc asked, her fingers tapping her sword hilt excitedly.

'Steady, girl. As you saw there are still many of them, about a hundred; far too many for even the likes of us to beat in a straight-up fight. They have no rules or common code and do as they like, even among their own kind, so it might be difficult for us to predict their moves. No! We need to gather more information about their habits, weapons and numbers. We need to know when they sleep, what they eat, everything. And we need to know about their leader and where the slaves are kept in the day. Then we are going to need a plan, an absolutely outrageous plan.'

'Should we make camp close by, Cap, and set up our scout detail?' Slemp asked. Silvaran nodded and they all got to work.

CHAPTER EIGHTEEN

Der awoke to the sound of whirring. Glancing around, she wrestled with her memory, trying to make sense of her dark surroundings. The noise was getting louder and a flashing of coloured lights from the other side of the room caught her eye.

The recollection of her surroundings slowly returned like the first flood of sunrise. She sat up, remembering the metal room, and then the lights blinked back on, crisp clean light that filled even the darkest of corners in the room.

Skoots stirred next to her. 'Wake up, narbo!' she said with a grin. His eyes flickered and he grimaced as the bright light tore through his sleepy state.

'Oh, that happened!' Skoots said, remembering the crazy day they had been through. He turned his head towards Der. 'Who you calling narbo… narbo!'

Der looked a little taken aback that he had failed to come back with his own insult and simply reused hers. 'Is that the best you can come up with?' she said with a grin.

'Oh, bag your face!' Skoots replied. They both sat

giggling for a while, till silence began to creep in again and they soon found themselves excitedly exploring the room.

A little beyond the desk was something that Der and Skoots never ever thought they would see beyond the fragments of old magazines and books.

'A sofa!' Skoots blurted out. He belted over to it in excitement, skidding to a stop on the shiny metallic floor. Then he tentatively turned round and lowered himself onto it. There was a groaning as the sofa that had spent many a year kicking back, enjoying a carefree life, suddenly had to support someone's weight.

A blissful look submerged Skoots' face and his mouth slowly opened in surprise.

'What's it like, Skoots?' Der asked.

'It's… It's… Sooo…'

'It's so… what?' Der pushed.

'Sorry, it's soo comfortable. You have to try it.'

Der wandered over and slowly lowered herself onto the sofa next to him. Soon both were captivated by the comfortable softness.

After a while, Der slowly turned her head towards Skoots and muttered, 'I could sleep on this, right now.'

Skoots looked over. 'I know and to think we spent the night sitting, sleeping against that hard metal door, when this amazing invention was here all along.'

They both giggled and leaned back nestling into the deep cushions. The humming of the tech in the room and the blissful comfort swept over like a soporific wave. Their eyelids, began to feel heavy and their minds sailed, when suddenly Der's stomach let out an angry and disputing grumble. The sound echoed around the room like a pack of monsters roaring to each other.

'I think it is time to eat!' said Der. Skoots needed no persuasion and they both jumped up off the sofa, causing the fragile old threads of the cushions to rip a little.

'Ouch, we just destroyed a priceless museum piece!' Skoots said trying to pull the two halves of the cushion cover back together.

'Yes, I guess we could have been a bit gentler getting up. It's just that I can't even remember the last time that I ate!' Der said rushing over to the door. 'Let's get everything from the ship and bring it all in. Then we can camp out here for a few days and explore the place. Bagsy the unripped side of the sofa to sleep tonight!'

After a couple of arduous trips to their trusty ship outside they were soon sitting back on the sofa and tucking into a variety of dried insects. They ate in silence gobbling down great mouthfuls.

Finally, their eating subsided, and they decided to explore the rest of the room. They gently stood up and walked a little further around the room, till they reached another sliding door. It was robust looking, but smaller than the one they had entered through, with a thick round glass panel about the size of a dinner plate.

They peered in to see what was beyond, but it was pitch black inside.

'Where do you think this leads to?' Skoots asked.

Der looked around for a handle or button and sure enough, to the right of the door, there was a small button.

'Let's find out!' she said, pressing it eagerly. The door slid open with a grinding and whirring, as if in protest.

As it completed its lethargic sequence, there was a beep and a series of bright lights lit up what appeared to be a short corridor of shiny metal, with two doors on either side and one right at the end.

Der and Skoots turned to each other, their faces lit up in excitement, and tentatively stepped into the corridor. It was just wide enough for them to stand side by side. The ceiling, arched from one wall to the other, fairly high above their heads. Along the edge of the floor, there were a series of lights that lit the way, the reflections emulated and bounced off the shiny metal. After two more timid steps they were level with the first two doors, one on each side.

They both turned to look at the first door on their left. At the push of a button, the door slid open to reveal a small room with a low ceiling, made from the same seemingly rust-proof metal. Along the far walls were three comfortable folding beds.

Standing with their backs to the strange beds, they could see that the walls either side of the sliding door were covered in cubbyhole shelves, from floor to ceiling. They were made from a shiny white substance and were almost empty.

‘So, this must have been some kind of bedroom. I wonder what this complex was used for?’ Skoots said matter-of-factly.

‘Ah your guess is as good as mine!’ Der replied while rummaging through the shelves and finding two identical adult size jackets made of a thick and durable grey fabric. The grey was accentuated by a black line down each side and on the left top pocket, there was a round logo which read *WRRC*.

Der also found a faded photograph depicting a family of four: a tall thin man wearing an identical jacket to the one they had found, standing beside a woman with kind eyes, her arm around him. Two children stood in front, smiling, their eyes clear and bright. In the background was a small wooden house with a lush green garden.

‘Look, that’s how people used to live years ago, outside and above ground. Look at the personal greenery!’ Skoots exclaimed.

‘Yes, it looks idyllic doesn’t it. I think they used to call the green spaces gardens,’ Der declared. ‘Amazing to think that green areas were so abundant that people could just have one around their house for enjoyment.’

Der slipped her arms into one of the jackets, causing Skoots to chuckle. The arms were far too long for her and hung down to her thighs.

‘Should we explore the next room?’ Der asked, raising an extremely long arm towards the door. The cuff of the jacket hung down and her pointing hand was completely lost to a bundle of fabric.

'Yes! Once you take that jacket off,' Skoots blurted out between uncontrollable giggles. Der reluctantly took it off and placed it caringly on the bed.

They wandered back to the corridor and tried the opposite room. Along the whole back wall was a large metal desk, its surface a disorganised mess of wires and odd boxes. In the centre of the desk, at arm's reach, stood a separate large box, its front covered in switches and dials, with a display readout showing several bars and graphs.

The back of the box was a spaghetti of more cables connected to whole piles of other devices, some with dials, and others with lights. To the left of the main central box was a flat control panel with sliders set at different positions.

Der extended a hand to try one of the sliders and Skoots exclaimed, 'What are you doing? That might do something horrid, like drop water on us, or cook us.'

'I'm not completely sure what it does, but am very sure it doesn't shower, or cook us,' Der said following that intuitive feeling she often got around electronics.

She tried one of the sliders, but nothing happened, so she returned it to the original position and moved to the next. Suddenly a crisp voice boomed out of a speaker somewhere in the room.

It was the same signal they had received on Der's makeshift radio, with the simple looped message: 'Look to the moon.'

'Well, this is certainly where the signal came from,

but I've no idea what it means. Let's carry on exploring,' Der suggested. 'Maybe we can find out what this place is, and that might give us a clue about the meaning of that broadcast.'

The next door on the left opened onto a sparse room with a long work-surface and lots of cupboards. Der noticed a sink, and intuitively rushed over, her hand bypassing her brain. There was a gush of water as she turned on a tap. She pushed it back in panic and the flow stopped.

'Water! And clean at that!' Skoots exclaimed. 'Look at this!' he declared a moment later, holding up a plate. 'This is what oldies used to eat on, look how shiny and colourful they are.'

Der found a drawer, and sliding it open she gasped as she saw lots of silver items. 'Look, these are what oldies used to eat with.'

'This stuff beats bits of foraged wood and metal. We're going to eat in style later, Der!' Skoots announced. After a good rummage through the cupboards they decided to check out the next room.

The door to this room was similar to the others, but with a bright green lighted button which was used to open it. When Der pushed the button, the circle turned red, and the door swished open. They glanced around, disappointed. It was hardly big enough for both of them to stand in. There was some kind of drainage on the floor, and immediately in front of them was a low seat-like object with several buttons on the back.

Der jabbed at the first button and to her utter surprise the seat shot up, folding neatly against the back to reveal a container with a tiny pool of water at the bottom.

Skoots bent down and contemplated testing the water. As he reached out his cupped hand to test it, Der grabbed his hand, and shouted, 'Stop! I think I know what this is and it isn't for drinking!' He paused, waiting for her to explain.

'Erm, this is for erm…' she hesitated. 'OK, so you know when you have to um, you know?'

'Have to drink quickly?' Skoots suggested, re-extending his hand.

'NO! Don't do that. Honestly, you'll regret it.'

'It's strange, but from all of the books I've read, I've never come across a mention of one of these,' Skoots said completely baffled.

'You won't, because many books don't like to mention about the 'bodily functions' of the heroes and heroines. They don't very often eat, and they don't ever, ever… um, how can I put this.' Der tilted her head.

'OK got it, you know in Fringetown, every so often, there is a room to er…' She still struggled. 'OK, you know the stinky rooms in Fringetown?' Der asked.

Skoots' eyebrows shot up. 'No, it isn't… is it?' he asked, not wanting to hear the answer.

'Yep,' Der confirmed. 'And when you finish you can…' she pressed another button. There was a loud gurgle and water washed the inside of the object.

Der glanced at the other buttons and wondered what

they did, but decided that was really was enough on *that* topic. As they backed away, the lid swished back down automatically.

'So, in olden days, is that how they…?' Skoots began.

'Yep,' she confirmed. 'Beats the stink rooms any day doesn't it?' They strode out of the door and just as it started to close, a gush of water began to spray from the ceiling and walls, cleaning the whole small room behind them.

'How very clean!' Skoots said as they turned to the final door.

Inside was another small room, about the size of the bedroom, but here the metal flooring had been covered almost from edge to edge with what once had been a thick blue fluffy rug. Der ran her toes through the ancient piles. It was soft and tickled the arch of her feet a little.

'Mmm, that is so soft!' she exclaimed. Skoots did the same and both of them became fixated by the soft, warm tickle on their feet and toes. Eventually after the novelty had worn off a bit, they decided to look around the room.

To one side was a small sofa, similar to the one in the main room. The rest of the room was taken up by shelves that covered all the walls, from floor to ceiling. Their mouths dropped wide open, like a couple of fish filter-feeding.

'Books,' Skoots muttered. They scanned shelf after shelf and sure enough there were hundreds of books and magazines. Next to the sofa was a small wooden table with a messy pile of books and manuals, presumably from the last person to have been there, a long, long time ago.

'Hang on…' Der said rushing to the door.

'Where are you going?' Skoots asked, raising his eyebrow.

'I need to go and see a man about a dog,' she replied.

'What?'

'You know, I want to go and spend a penny!'

'What?' he said in an even more baffled tone.

'Nature is calling,' she tentatively tried.

'WHAT?' Skoots shouted, completely baffled.

'I need to go and do that thing you've never read about, you know in that room next door!' she said feeling far too embarrassed at the level of explanation she was needing to give. And without further discussion, she opened the door and left.

Several minutes later she returned, to find Skoots still looking a little bewildered. 'How was it?' Skoots asked.

'Umm, usually, that isn't a question one would ask another. But, yes, it was far better than the stink rooms in Fringetown, and beats bushes, or rocks any day,' Der detailed. At that, Skoots turned and strode towards the door.

'Where are you going now?' Der asked.

'Um…' he replied. 'Next door, to the man and dog.'

He returned a few minutes later with a look of relief and his hair completely soaked.

'It's so much more comfortable and civilised than what our people do. These oldies really were smart. Though I haven't quite got the hang of the buttons yet.' Der looked at his dripping hair and burst out laughing. Skoots tried to dry his scraggly hair with his jacket, till it stopped dripping.

'Look at all of these books!' Der gestured.

'I know, right. I could stay here for months reading them!' Skoots said with a gigantic grin on his face.

'I'm pretty sure your mum would twig by then, that you're actually not in Fringetown, and are off on a dangerous adventure with me. She would hunt you down!' Der reminded him. Skoots let out a gulp at the thought.

Der sat down gently on the sofa and inspected the pile of books left on the table beside her.

Skoots sat next to her as Der picked up the book on top of the pile and tried to make out the faded title. *The WWRC Habitation and Operation Manual.* They traced their fingers around the large, capitalised letters *WWRC.*

It was bound in a cream material, and other than the title, the cover was completely plain. The spine slightly creaked as they opened the cover to reveal the first page and they felt that familiar smell of old books wash over them like a wave. There were some names of people who had contributed to the book and a lot of white space; they flipped over to the next page.

Skoots decided to read, as he thought he was the most experienced in 'oldie' text. He read it aloud.

'Introduction to the WWRC. WWRC stands for Weather Warning Research Centre.'

They looked at each other in excitement. 'That's it! That's what this place was used for. The weather?' The word seemed to stir some long-forgotten memory for Der.

'But what is weather?' Skoots questioned, his face the picture of puzzlement. Der scoured her broken memory for a tangible meaning of the word, but it all felt so distant and scattered.

Skoots read on in silence and after a while he looked up and explained.

'In olden days the weather changed throughout most days. There were hot times, cold times, dry times and sometimes water fell from the sky. Even my people have witnessed this rare occurrence, but during the olden days, it was more common. These different temperatures and conditions they referred to as "the weather". Nowadays we live underground, so we don't think about weather. Desert travellers think of the winds that their sails can catch every night, but that's about it.'

'Wind. Ah yes,' Der said as she pondered the word. 'The Virdarians know of that too; their trees sway in it sometimes and maybe even break.' She thought back to that night in Golderwin's tree, realising how long ago even that seemed now.

'There were also violent types of weather,' Skoots began as he read further on, but Der cut him off.

'Well it sounds a little boring to me!' Der said, as her

eyes caught glimpse of the next book down on the pile, *The Adventures of the Daring Rider.*

'Now *that's* more *my* kind of book,' she exclaimed, snatching it up and opening it at page one. It was hard going at first, but the words and settings were strangely familiar and the more she read the faster she got.

Soon they had slipped off into equally engrossing worlds as they sat deep in their books, the silence only broken by the sliding sound of paper on paper as the pages turned. They stretched out their feet onto the soft rug in front of them, the only physical reminder of their surroundings.

The rest of the day slipped by, until late in the afternoon when they emerged from their books, or rather were pulled rudely away, by a synchronised chorus of stomach rumbles.

'Let's eat,' Skoots declared, and they both strolled out, books still in their hands, to prepare their dinner.

A while later and the smells of delicious cooked critters hung in the air. They sat on the sofa in the main room, tucking into their food in complete style with the forks and the plates they had found in the kitchen.

'I could totally stay here for a while to read, it has everything we need!' Der said turning to Skoots for his approval.

'Me too, Der, this manual on the WWRC is really interesting; it tells you everything you need to know about this building and weather systems. It was built –

from what I can understand – before our civilisation moved underground, at a time when weather had become erratic and dangerous, so the centre was designed to give people an early warning system for events like adverse storms.'

'Storms?' she questioned. Another word that was strangely familiar to Der, but she couldn't quite remember why.

'Yes, I think there might be some pictures here of different types of storms. Look, this is a snowstorm – it brought a kind of solid water, piling it up like the sand dunes in our desert.' He pointed to an image of thick drifts of snow and dark black clouds.

'And what kind of storm is this?' Der asked, pointing to a faded photograph of a lightning storm.

Skoots stared at the photo, tracing the blue lines of lightning with his finger. A thought passed into his mind as he connected two seemingly unrelated things.

'This could destroy a ship, right? And this could be described as… blue fire!' he muttered aloud. Both turned to each other and uttered the words, 'The Fulgur.'

Der pondered this. 'Is it possible that your… I mean *our* people once saw these rare lightning storms? And because so few saw them over the years and even less lived to tell the tale, the tale evolved into a legendary monster that wanders the desert, devouring everything in its path.'

Skoots puzzled over the thought of such a simple

explanation for the legendary Fulgur. After a while though, the novelty of solving a local legend wore off on Der, and she soon found herself back in her fictional book of a heroine, yet again saving the day.

Skoots grinned at his friend's contented face and opened his own book again, only pausing to utter, 'We have to be ready for the lights to go off when the sun goes down!'

Der managed to mutter a carefree melodic, 'Yeah,' which tapered off like a sigh.

CHAPTER NINETEEN

It had been quite a few days since they had discovered the small library, and each day they had agreed to stay just 'a little' longer. It had taken them a while to get used to the fact that when the sun went down, the doors locked and the lights flickered off.

But they now had a system. They would eat, drink and use the 'place at the end of the corridor', as much as they needed in the daytime, and shortly before sundown they would be settled down in the main room.

Skoots had brought the large rug into the main room and had spread out across it several other reference books that were mentioned in the manual.

He sat in the centre with an arc of books all open at different pages, flitting from one to another, as different details were mentioned.

Turning another page of the manual, he recognised a familiar image. He let out a gasp. 'Look at this, Der!' he exclaimed with almost explosive enthusiasm.

Der reluctantly pulled herself away from a scene in her book. She rolled her eyes in annoyance and raised her eyebrows to beckon Skoots to speak quickly, so that she could get back to the action-packed scene. When Skoots spoke, it came thick and fast in a blurt of excitement.

'Look at this image. Do you recognise it?' he said pointing to the round desk with its five black screens.

'Yes, I have been meaning to have a tinker with that. But just can't stop reading these books, I don't know why they are so addictive,' she said

Without even acknowledging her reply, he continued, 'That's the OFC, the main "Observation and Forecast Computer". It displays all the readings and helps the scientists record, predict and monitor the weather. Isn't that exciting!' he said, barely breathing between words.

'Fascinating!' Der said in a rather dismissive and sarcastic tone, before lowering her eyes back to her book.

A little later, her eyes flashed up when she saw Skoots get up and walk in the direction of the OFC. He tentatively sat in the swivel chair, amazed by the wheels sliding effortlessly across the polished metal floor.

He laid his books out on the desk in front of him, a finger to his mouth in contemplation. 'Ahh,' he muttered as he pointed to the round object. 'A mouse! Strange, it doesn't look like a rodent,' he mumbled to himself, jiggling it from side to side.

A loud whir from under the desk spun up and some lights flickered. The black screens fizzled into life and brought up a circle with the words 'initiating wakeup sequence'. Then the screens burst into colour, showing a pattern of curved and wavy lines overlapped with coloured blocks.

He studied the screen and referred to several pages of different books. He moved the mouse tentatively, his eyes following the corresponding object on the screen – a bright fluorescent pink arrow. 'The only colour not included in the readouts,' he muttered, recalling a detail he had read.

He played with the novelty of his movements being echoed by the arrow on the screen, shifting it right and left, up and down abruptly, as if trying to catch it out or outsmart it. Eventually the novelty began to wear off and he decided to get to work identifying the items, buttons and areas of each screen he had read about in the books and manuals. He muttered words like 'time', 'atmospheric pressure', 'humidity', and a whole bunch of technical words that would be lost on most people unless they had had enough enthusiasm to spend weeks or more reading dry manuals about meteorological science.

He felt something pushing on the back of his chair and noticed that Der had torn herself away from her book to see what he was doing. 'Oh, how's the book?' Skoots asked, curious about her sudden presence and interest in what he was doing.

'Finished it. I'm bored now, so thought I would show you how to use this tech! So scoot, Skoots.' She grinned, expecting him to 'scoot' over and let her use it.

'Thanks, sis, but I know how to use this now. I read

the manuals,' he said with an air of triumph on his face. 'Look, this is the centre, here, and these lines show the valley we sailed down.' He gestured towards the screen.

'This is a map of the area that comes from satellites, large gadgets that orbit the earth. I don't know how or why they are all still functioning, up there, but they are! This is real data, look,' he exclaimed, swishing the mouse around, and the screen zoomed out to show a much larger view.

They both squinted at the different areas that they recognised. 'That must be Fringetown!' Der exclaimed excitedly as he flicked the mouse expertly and zoomed even further out.

'That's Cockroach Alley! And that's the entrance to Balldock!' she said, pointing to the other side of the screen.

With a few more flicks the screen zoomed even further out and Der caught sight of a little oasis of green, completely surrounded by the desert. It looked like a tiny island encircled by an ocean of sand, the great dune waves leering up high, threatening to wash over it.

'Can you zoom in?' she asked. A flick and a swish and they were looking at the green island. 'It seems much smaller than I remember it. That's the Virdarians' village. I'm sure it used to be much further from the edge.'

Skoots glanced over towards the other screens which displayed lists of data and superimposed maps. He read the screens carefully, referring to his books. 'Look, this means that the temperature is high today and the humidity is extremely low,' he said, attempting to explain the various columns of data and how he had come to that conclusion.

'OK, but I could have looked outside to tell you that,' she replied, failing to see the point. 'In fact, we know it will be hot and dry, because that's more or less the constant, er… what did you call it? Weather?'

'Yes, that's a fair point. The map is useful though, and we could zoom out even further than our people have ever explored! We can use it to explore our land without actually moving, and also see what the weather will be like over the next few days, which I guess will be… hot and dry!' he said with a smile, as his hand hovered over the mouse. He clicked the button and instantly it displayed the weather for the next day.

'Hmm,' he said as he looked down the list of data. 'Yep! Dry and hot!' he confirmed.

'Wow! That's some amazing prediction there!' Der said with a strong odour of sarcasm. 'Does it even still work?'

'Of course, it works. Look!' he said defensively, flicking back through the sets of data. 'Here we can see that tomorrow night will be slightly hotter and more humid than tonight. And the night after that will be even more humid and there will be very little wind at night. So, no it isn't broken!' he said matter-of-factly.

'OK, so what about later this week. Dry?' she said with a smirk.

'Yep, here we are. As we can see, it will be… what?'

Skoots stopped mid-sentence, gawping at the screens like a plankton-feeder. 'What's that?' he muttered in terror, pointing to a new blob on the main screen and flicking his head towards the data on the others.

'Oh, that is odd. The humidity will increase. The pressure looks like it will drop abruptly. Hang on…' he said, mostly to himself as he zoomed out further on the map.

'What's that?' he said in a frantic voice, pointing to a giant red swirl surrounded by yellow and orange tails, which they had only seen a small part of on the previous view.

'That isn't supposed to be there.'

'So, what's the big deal, bruv, some red and yellow stuff might be pretty to look at. We should go and watch it in the sky!' Der replied, unconcerned.

'Er, no! You don't understand, Der. This is bad, really bad. It's absolutely unheard of. Look.' He reached for a book on clouds and weather systems and flicked through expertly, his fingers a blur till he reached a page with a similar satellite image. 'Look at this!' He pushed it sharply in front of Der's nose. She looked closely at the image and read the various blocks of text aloud.

Hurricanes and cyclones are forms of weather systems that can cause great risk to infrastructure. They come with heavy winds and usually large amounts of precipitation. Der stopped reading, still not quite understanding.

'So it's going to be windy and wet. Well, that is super rare, but we could do with some water, right?'

'Let me look at the numbers, to see how big it will be,' Skoots said, glancing at the screens and cross-referencing them in his books. 'Ah, no, no, that can't be right,' he said, slumping further back in his seat.

'What's wrong?' Der asked.

'Well the 'mbar' is 850, and the size is—'

He didn't get a chance to finish his detailed explanation, because Der interrupted him abruptly with, 'I don't understand all this "weather" speak. Now stop gibbering and tell me in simple language *what is wrong*?' she demanded.

'OK, in olden days there were different types of storms. Some like the Fulgur which were small and not too powerful, although still devastating to ships. Others that were much bigger and stronger were labelled as hurricanes! These hurricanes are not like regular storms, they could bring so much rain and wind, they could... well do this.' He turned the page to images of flooding, showing whole towns and cities destroyed.

'And this one here that the screen predicts,' he said as he pointed to the red symbol on the screen, 'is a mega storm. It will be unbelievably strong.'

Skoots clicked the mouse a couple of times to show the trajectory of the storm and both their faces filled with terror.

'So, what this computer is saying is that the hurricane will approach near here?' Der said, pointing to a patch of desert just beyond the forest. 'And then directly cross the forest, travel through the desert and pass right over

Balldock? What do you think the risks are?'

'Well, this sized storm could easily topple trees or whole forests,' Skoots replied. 'And the sheer amount of rain might run down all the tunnels into Balldock, completely flooding it. Anyone left inside could be injured, or even die. And anyone outside... well, they wouldn't even stand a chance. But it's difficult to predict how many trees will topple and how many people will die.'

Der sunk down to her knees and started to think of her dear friend Golderwin and the kind but fearsome people in Balldock. Tears trickled down her face as she imagined the forest being torn apart and Balldock flooded. A warm arm curled around her shoulders as Skoots hugged her.

'I'm sorry, Der,' he said with tear-filled eyes. 'There's nothing we can do to stop the hurricane. But we do know that both our people and the Virdarians are strong and resourceful, so certainly some might survive.'

'Is there nothing we can do to help them, nothing at all?' Der half cried and half spoke, her matted hair soaked with tears.

'Well this station can't stop the weather, only predict it so that...' They looked at each other and spoke in unison. 'So that people have an early warning system!'

Der dried her eyes and brushed her matted hair off her face, then stood up with a new look of determination. 'You said this station was built to give people an early warning of severe weather. Well let's use it for just that! We have to warn them, so that they can find a place that's safe before the mega storm hits.'

Skoots stood to join her. 'It would be dangerous trying to get all the way to Balldock and the forest from here in just a few days. And not to mention we would have to be crazy to sail towards a major storm; most would run the other way to safety.'

'And worse,' Der added. 'If the storm, Cockroaches, snakes and pirates don't kill us, your mum will!'

'So… Dangerous and crazy… sounds like us all over,' Skoots agreed. 'When do we leave?'

'Well, let's read a few more books from the library, have a few days to sleep and then have a clean-up in here for a couple of days, before we discuss our plan for a few days more!' Der said with a gigantic smirk on her face.

'Tonight, it is then!' Skoots replied, grinning. 'We have a few hours till sundown. Right, we need to pack essentials, and look on the computer map for a place that might be used to shelter the people of the forest and Balldock. Oh, and let's get some paper and trace the maps on the screen so we can use them to plot the fastest course.'

Several hours later, and a slightly tired and very apprehensive Der and Skoots placed the final pack of supplies into the small and agile desert ship. They glanced back up to the weather station with a fond smile, and in the last fraying strips of sunlight that slipped over the tops of the cliffs, they raised the sails.

Der tapped the map she had used to plot their course. 'Two days, if we hustle hard and sail at full speed. Remember we rest here.' She pointed to a cave they had found on the computer, that was perfect as a stopover about halfway.

Skoots patted the vehicle affectionately. 'I know we'll be asking a lot of you, girl, to sail at full speed nonstop, but please hold together for us. We've got to make it, we have to!'

Der smiled gently and looked him deep in the eyes. 'If we don't make it, thanks for being the closest to family I have ever had and for being my ride or die.'

Skoots said nothing, but a few tears trickled from his eyes as he hugged her. 'OK, BFF, let's do this. Let's sail like there is no tomorrow!'

With the flick of a lever the sails billowed out into the wind, and the roar of the DMAD cranked to full filled the air. They lurched forward, the sheer force sending Der and Skoots jolting backwards in their seats.

Soon the ship was hurtling down the valley as fast as they could push it, the frame creaking and groaning, and the mast rumbling in the wind which ruffled their hair around violently. They had to work hard to keep the steering straight and true, and the hair from their sore watering eyes. Their ears rang with a whistling sound as the craft cut through the air.

CHAPTER TWENTY

Songs of defiance and anger echoed through what was left of the forest, bouncing to and fro, as a circle of Virdarians stood among the secluded clump of trees that was once their home. Their heads were bowed, eyes filled with tears that trickled down over their rough rugged cheeks. At their feet lay a fallen woman.

Sitting at her side, refusing to move, rocking to and fro, was Golderwin, his eyes as red as the winter morning sky. He howled a song over and over again, almost unaware of the surrounding village and its people. The whole forest lay in silence that night, except for his harrowing howls and the heated songs of his people.

Gladerwin stepped towards Golderwin and put a hand on his shoulder. He said nothing for a moment or two, in silent consolation. Then with a new determination he addressed the whole village in the singing language of the Virdarians.

'They have gone too far this time. Flosorwin was defending the forest, just like you all, when the pirates attacked. What have the times come to, when our people die protecting the last trees in this world? Look over there,' he sung in a raging voice, pointing to the edge of the forest that they could now see from their village.

'Even in all the great wars our ancestors fought, has the forest edge ever been as close? Today, one of our own beloved citizens has fallen, protecting her home. The pirates don't even take the wood anymore. They just leave it blackened and broken on the forest floor. And at such a pace, we are only weeks away from the last tree.

'We have tolerated each other's civilisations for a long time, but this time they have gone too far. They have left us with no home, no future, and most importantly, no options. We must go to all-out war, to avenge the fallen and to stop the final trees from falling. If we do not act today, there will be no tomorrow for us, or for this forest!'

The last of his song ignited a pure fire into the hearts of the crowd. One by one they stepped forward, putting their hands on their hearts and a great roaring song went up.

'War! War! War!'

As Gladerwin turned to leave the village, he stopped by an ancient tree with a great wooden door, and produced an old key that had hung around his neck since he was only a boy. He gazed at it deeply, reflecting for a moment on its history.

He had hoped that he would never have to use the key, much like his father and grandfather. Yet here he was. And despite the grand, fiery speech, he regretted that it had come to this.

He gave out a sigh, long and melodic. Then taking a last look at the pitted, blackened key, slotted it into the timeless keyhole and turned it with a screech. The lock almost seemed to be protesting. The heavy door had been closed for an age and he had to grasp it with both hands, pulling with all his might. Eventually it creaked open, leaving him panting, the years showing.

When he turned to enter the tree, he felt a hand on his shoulder. It was Brookorwin, his wife. 'There must be another way, dear?' she sang, her eyes filled will pain and sorrow.

'I'm afraid not, my love,' he said solemnly. 'Sometimes we must fight for what we love. For our people and, more importantly, for the last few trees of the last forest in our world.'

He entered the tree and returned with an ancient hoard of spears, swords and great bags of equipment, which he piled high. He gazed on the weapons of their ancestors that had not seen the light of day for centuries, items that should have no place in their task of tending to the forest, and his eyes welled up with tears.

Then he glanced back to the distant edges of the forest and his eyes narrowed. 'Arm yourselves!' he shouted. 'We are at war! We march on Balldock immediately. We will destroy their tech and teach them to never return to the forest. FOR THE LAST FOREST!' The booming voice of his song seemed to shake the very trees.

One by one, the villagers marched up to the pile and selected weapons and equipment. And less than an hour later, the men and women of the village were marching through the last of the trees and out into the desert night.

When they reached the sand, they glanced back at the strange, decimated trees, left blackened and broken around the edge of the forest. Then they turned without a word and began their long march across the dunes. Their strides, unlike in the forest, where they treaded delicately and calculated the damage of each step, were large and determined. Only the few children were left behind, and Golderwin, who remained kneeling, howling at his wife's side.

***

Balldock was bustling as normal with traders, pirates, merchants, cooks and all manner of people hurrying around. People came here from far off towns and villages to find a job, tout for work, sell their wares, or rest between journeys. The usual pirate suspects were there, and a few new faces too, all tolerating each other, for the sake of the rules. Out there in the desert, there were no rules. But here in Balldock, the great melting pot of the Wastelands, there was a treaty of peace. Vendettas were left at the door.

The lights on the desert slope flickered as a craft approached. It was something that happened often in the night, but there was something wrong with the approach of this particular ship. Usually they slowed as they rolled down the steep slope, but this ship struggled to even stay in a straight line, buffeting the sides of the tunnel.

The sails and mast were smashed and torn, and a huge hole had been ripped in the side of the ship. The remainder of the crew were in a mess, once formidable pirates, now covered in blood, shouting chaotically as the ship hurtled out of control into the entrance of the main arena.

A man was slumped over the wheel, wrestling to keep it on course between blackouts. He mustered just enough strength to pull a lever and engage the brakes, as the ship smashed into some barriers and came to a splintery halt beside one of the jetties.

Two men staggered and fumbled to drop the gangplank, one of them falling there and then. Only one man managed to make it off the gangplank, dragging a broken and smashed leg and covered in gashes all over.

His eyes flickered weakly as he laboured over every step he took, and reaching the bottom of the plank, he collapsed into the arms of two watchmen. Others soon dashed over and managed to bandage up his worst wounds and bring the man round. The lone survivor of the formidable Blood Gang began to mutter his tale.

'We were sailing out to the forest to fell one or two

trees for the village of Sandford. They needed the wood to make struts for their main tunnel entrance that had a partial collapse last week. It was supposed to be a simple and lucrative run. But the Foresters were waiting for us.

'They accused us of cutting down fifty trees. We tried to explain that we'd only just arrived and just needed one or two trees to save a small village many moons away. But they kept saying that we were responsible for all the burnt trees.

'We tried to reason with them, but it got heated and before we knew it, there was a scuffle. But it escalated, and by the end two of my men were dead and one of theirs. The rest was a blur of violence until more of them turned up and we fled.'

By now a large crowd had gathered to investigate the disturbance, though only those at the front could hear the faint words of the last of the Blood Gang, as his whispered words finally faded into silence. A man next to him gently shook his arm.

'Hey, come on, don't die on us.' But it was too late. Only a few had heard the words, but soon the people behind them were clawing to hear. The story was soon being recounted.

'They went to the forest for a single tree to save the whole of Sandford and were met by vicious Foresters that attacked them and killed their crew.'

By the time the story reached the back of the crowd, it had been exaggerated further. 'The heroic crew were saving all the lives of the people in Sandford from the barbaric Foresters. They fought valiantly, but the Foresters were too well armed.' And so the story evolved, rippling out into the crowd and on into every corner of Balldock.

Some stories can inspire; some can push us to transcend our fears and differences; some even to reach for the stars, but I am sorry to say that this one simply fed the dark monster of hatred. It stoked up the whispers in people's hearts of their age-old hatred for the Foresters, a vehicle for blame for people's disgruntled lives, their struggles and their poverty.

In a mere moment, the whole town had been stirred up into a restless fury. Scarlan, a formidable and legendary pirate, saw her opportunity. She stood on the prow of her ship, her long scar glistening in the pale light and spoke out in a great booming voice. 'It's time to put a stop to the evil Foresters once and for all! We go to war! Who's with me?'

And in answer a pirate named Sabretooth, with a long beard and bushy orange eyebrows, stepped forward. He drew a long serrated sword and held it high above his head and with a blood-curdling yell cried, 'WARRRR!'

The bellow was taken up by others, one by one, as they stepped forward with weapons held high, the whole of Balldock shuddering with their cry. Pirates stood by traders, inn owners stood by shipwrights; foragers, growers and crafters, shoulder to shoulder, united with one aim.

And before they even had a chance to process what

they were doing, the army was gathered and ship after ship was launched out into the desert night, each filled to the very brim with a motley crew of anyone and everyone that wanted blood.

Soon a great armada was assembled before the entrance, line after line. And not just pirate ships. There were transporters, huge ships with bulbous hulls. There were sleek explorer ships, made for smuggling or scouting, and trade ships, designed to ferry goods or people from place to place. And then there were the pirate ships, which varied just as much in size and purpose, each one as unique as the crew that sailed it.

But now they stood together, bow to bow, hull to hull, crowded by a chanting crazed army. The sails went up and in one giant rumbling roar, the strong night wind filled the hundred sails, and the ships lurched forward like a great beast from the depths.

***

Just outside the forest, out of sight of the stomping Virdarians, four lone ships stood with their lights out, in absolute silence. The moon was blotted out by a swirling wisp of cloud, and in the cover of the darkened dunes four faces smiled in a triumphant display.

The formidable but elegant Satisa leant into the group, whispering in a smooth and satisfied tone, 'Well done, looks like our hard work has finally paid off!'

'Yes, Satisa,' said Trode, his eye twitching. 'According to our spies the Foresters have taken up arms and are marching across the dunes to war as we speak.'

Dorlan grinned behind his voluminous beard. 'And it seems only a few of the gullible Blood Gang made it out of the battle alive. According to my sources, they riled the whole of Balldock into war, just as we planned. And they too are marching.'

'It was a fine idea, paying groups to log, feeding people sob stories and tipping off old Scarlan,' Style said, rubbing his hands.

'It certainly was!' Growser agreed.

'Right, let's hold back here and let the Foresters and Wastelanders take care of each other. And when they are done, we will enslave or finish off anyone left,' Satisa said, her eyes glinting.

'Then the forest will be ours!' Growser whispered, her club resting on her shoulder.

***

Balldock lay eerily silent that night, like a ghost town, almost empty of ships and without a soul in sight. The whispering silence was suddenly broken by a small lone ship that came in hot, flying deftly down the slope and screeching to a halt by the closest docking plank.

It was once an elegant and legendary ship, known by all, but now it appeared that time and conflict had finally caught up with it – just like its captain, who single-handedly dropped the gangplank.

He gestured to eight young Virdarians aboard to stay on his ship. He strolled off standing tall, but feeling broken, and walking with a slight limp, his tricorn hat barely on his head, and his worse for wear waistcoat missing most of his instruments, covering up his bruised and lacerated torso.

Across one eye there was a fresh cut, deep and raw. His eye was permanently closed and probably blinded. His good eye flashed around the empty place, still filled with fire and strength as he paced along the boardwalks, a look of suspicion on his face, and a hand firmly placed on the pommel of his trusty sword.

Just then he turned his head in the direction of the entrance, as a loud rumbling noise echoed down the tunnel. Something was flying down the slope at double speed.

The ship sped down the slopes, two sets of hands firmly grasping the controls, grappling to keep the vehicle under control.

'Almost there, Skoots! Remember, stick with me, Balldock can be dangerous. We have to warn them quickly and then get to the forest!' Der battled to get her voice above the shouting of the DMAD, the sails, and the echoing tunnel.

Skoots nodded, and then catching a glimpse of the bottom, they hit the brakes, sliding across the centre of the docks. Smoke and dust churned up everywhere in a spectacular entrance. As the deft ship finally and reluctantly stopped, they glanced around the dock. Der's face was filled with utter surprise to see the empty space.

‘Thought you said this was the hub of the desert. The melting pot of our people?’ Skoots said, an eyebrow raised.

‘It is… was,’ Der said puzzled.

Suddenly there was a loud and booming voice. ‘OOOY!’ Silvaran shouted, narrowing his eyes and drawing his sword. A second figure, Arc, dropped from the ship’s mast and was at his side in a flash, her sword drawn.

‘Silvaran! I am so glad to see you! There is danger coming!’ Der shouted.

Silvaran’s face wrinkled into a look of complete bewilderment. ‘What are you two doing here? It isn’t safe for you!’ he said in anger.

As Der and Skoots ran over, he and Arc sheathed their swords. ‘Cap, there is a hurricane, I mean…’

She thought for a way to explain quickly and continued. ‘The Fulgur is coming and it will hit the forest, then Balldock. The forest will be destroyed and Balldock flooded. We came to warn everyone,’ she blurted out.

Silvaran and Arc looked shocked at the mention of the Fulgur. ‘What? How do you know that?’ Silvaran asked.

Skoots looked his sister in the eyes. ‘Sis, we discovered a way to track the weather – I mean Fulgur. It’s a long story. But please just trust us. We don’t have much time.’

Arc looked deeply into her brother’s eyes and could

see the real fear in them. She turned to Silvaran. 'Cap, I believe him,' she said firmly.

'OK, we have to warn everyone. But more importantly, where is everyone?' he shouted, looking around.

'All gone to fight!' an equally booming voice echoed back.

'Grogen, you old sea dog!' Silvaran exclaimed, noticing a lone man approaching. The two quickly embraced.

'Silvaran, you have to do something,' he insisted. 'Everyone went crazy and left to sail to the forest and fight the Foresters. I refused to fight and stayed back to protect the kids.'

At once, eight young Virdarians were standing at Silvaran's side, their eyes filled with tears.

'Sir, we are in your gratitude for saving us from the Cockroaches. But please take us to our kind,' a young Virdarian adult said. 'If you can do anything to stop our people fighting and our forest from being destroyed, please,' he continued.

Silvaran glanced around with a sigh at all the expectant faces looking to him for the answer. 'OK, let's go. Grogen, you coming too?'

Grogen looked his old captain up and down, observing his wounds and cut face. 'Probably for the best, Cap, I wouldn't want you getting hurt!' he said with a slight grin.

'You'd best stay behind me, Grogen. That sword of

yours is rusty and blunt!' he replied with equal wit. He turned to Der and Skoots to tell them to stay behind, but they were already halfway up the slope in their ship. The two ships shot out into the moonlit sky.

It wasn't hard to track the armada, as there were so many marks all leading in the same direction. The 'V' sails went up and the *Dawn Eagle* soared ahead, skipping across the desert like its namesake.

Yet despite its plucky and legendary speed, a small and deft ship without lights sped past it, leaving the great captain in utter surprise. Der smiled as she and Skoots wrestled with their agile ship, imagining Silvaran's and Arc's faces as they were passed by the stealth ship.

CHAPTER TWENTY ONE

It was a calm night with very few clouds, the velvety sky punctured by thousands of glittering gemstones. The bright half moon shone radiantly, its craters clear and defined in the crisp night, and its silver beams dancing over the crests of the desert waves. Just above the horizon the second smaller moon, smooth and dull, shimmered faintly in the atmosphere.

A great thudding drumbeat of marching feet tore through the stillness of the desert night. Virdarians! All dressed in heavy war gear, bounding in unison, each stride making a crash that resonated from dune to dune. The rumbling cacophony was carried far off over the waves, only to collide with a relentless thundering grumble of hundreds of wheels.

As the great armada summited the crest of a particularly massive dune, and the Forest army reached the summit of an equally large dune adjacent, the air fell deadly silent.

A bitter wind swept through the sandy valley, lashing up sand and dust into their faces. Though it stung like fire, both sides remained unblinking, poised like statues. They stood locked in place like two great desert scorpions, their fingers twitching at their sides, their weapons calling to them.

The Virdarians stood in their magnificent armour, their eyes trained on their enemy. Their armour was fashioned from finely cut pieces of hardwood, stitched together to form a carapace-like covering, tough and flexible. On their heads, were flamboyant helmets of thick animal hide, hardened with forest buzz honey.

Some had huge swords that looked like they had been forged by forgotten smiths in times long gone by. Others bore long curved axes, their decorative blades glistening in the moonlight. And some held long metal-tipped spears, even taller than the Virdarians themselves.

Their beautiful suits of armour had been expertly crafted by the greatest artisans of their ancestors, yet they looked unnatural on these villagers. Many of them were too big, or badly fitting, while the equally well-fashioned weapons also looked oddly out of place in their hands. They clearly had never used them in their lifetimes. Some held them like gardening implements and others held them with tentative grips, wondering how to swing or use them. But despite their lack of experience, their hard stares were unwavering.

At last Gladerwin their leader stepped forward past

the crest, one step, then another, leaving his armour-clad forest people behind watching his every move.

'What are they doing?' a murmur went out in the ranks of the Wastelanders.

'Looks like he wants to speak!' the pirate with the bushy orange beard announced. He straightened his tricorn hat and brushed a wash of orange matted hair out of his face. His eyes narrowed and he stepped forward to the edge of his ship.

He was a tall lump of a man with broad shoulders and was wearing a well-kept green waistcoat that housed an assortment of tools and implements. Round his waist was a thick black belt fashioned from a rubbery material, which supported his jagged sword. He had fashioned the blade by hand long ago and it bore the marks of many a battle. On his other side hung a home-made telescope.

'Drop the gangplank, lads,' he growled. 'Let's see what this dumb Forester wants to talk about. Maybe they want to surrender!'

'But, Cap, what if he attacks you?' came a voice from the crowded deck.

'Then toothy here will have some fun! Cover me, lads, and if they make a move, carve 'em down!' He drew his barbaric weapon, smiling to his crew.

Just then a gritty growl came from an adjacent ship. 'Who made you the leader, old Sabretooth?' a thin and shabby-looking captain shouted. His ship was three times larger and was a boiling mass of people, all jostling for a place to see. While he waited for an answer, he narrowed his one good eye and scratched at an itch behind the patch on his other.

But before Sabretooth or his sword could answer, another pirate shouted, 'Oy, you bunch of soft bottom-feeders, if anyone should lead it should be me!'

A short and dumpy woman roared with anger as she swung around a large chunk of metal on the end of a chain, in a self-fashioned flail. She had a long scar that went from the top of her forehead all the way down to her knee, disappearing behind the lush velvety waistcoat and well-kept shorts. Her eyes were a milky steel blue and unwavering in the bold strength they conveyed. She whistled and a harpoon swivelled round to aim at Sabretooth's ship.

A silence swept across the valley again, as eyes glanced up and down at the great harpoon-laden ship and the massive woman standing bolt upright on its stern. But the glances all stopped short of her steely blue eyes. Every pirate knew that Captain Scarlan was not one to be meddled with. She was a legend, only superseded by Silvaran himself.

The silence was broken by Sabretooth, whose voice had changed from a gritty boom to a silky, wormy tone.

'Captain Scarlan, sorry. I… I didn't see you there. Of course, you would be our natural leader. I just thought if someone should step out in front of a barbaric Forester, then it should be someone… expendable; one of us lowly scum, not an important leader like yourself.' He lulled, his hands circling each other nervously.

A cold hard stare that could cut ships down shot across to Sabretooth, and his eyes dropped to the deck in a display of complete subservience. A bead of sweat trickled down his forehead disappearing behind the orange forest of eyebrows and beard. After a long silence, Captain Scarlan spoke.

'OK, small fry, go play chitchat with the Foresters! Hurry up and aggravate them though, because it is time for BLOOD!' her voice went up into a thundering roar.

The sapping walk from the end of the gangplank and down the dune to the centre of the valley below had felt like an age to Sabretooth.

He looked up into the Forester's eyes. They both had their weapons drawn and were resting on the hilts. From behind, hundreds of eyes watched through telescopes of varying size and accuracy. Those without telescopes had climbed a mast or jostled to the front to squint at the confrontation below.

Sabretooth glanced up at the towering Forester who stood a full foot above him and tried to read the air for the opening of their impending conversation.

'So,' he began, hoping that the tiny word would inspire the first step in their parley. The Forester narrowed his eyes and broke into a deep and resonating song. If Sabretooth could speak, or rather sing Virdarian, he might have found the points he made logical and fair. But sadly none of the pirates knew how to communicate with the Foresters. And as the rumbling melody carried on the wind, the pirates looked on, perplexed.

It seemed like the Foresters were mocking them, disregarding the strength of their mighty armada. The intricate tones of the Virdarian language were completely lost to them, and all it did was stoke the already roaring fire.

'You do know this is no time for singing,' Sabretooth growled. 'We are here to avenge the death of the Blood Gang and enforce our rights to the Forest's resources that we need to survive.'

The Forester made no reply, but from the dunes behind him a slow melody began echoing down as the whole village took up their song, a blended symphony of high notes and low rumbling tones. Their tunes skipped across the wind like a pebble on the sea, before finally dropping into the ocean with an explosion of ripples, enraging their enemies.

Sabretooth took a step back and raised his right eyebrow in utter disbelief. He had tried his best to stay calm, but now it seemed that the Foresters really were mocking them. This was too much.

'How dare they mock our people at a time like this,' he muttered to himself. And at that thought, something terrible took over, as the stories of their age-old rift began to bubble up inside him, magnified by the growing roar rising up from the ships behind. With a great roar, he seized his serrated sword, narrowed his eyes and in a clean and lightning-fast movement slashed the Forester across the arm and chest with such precision it cut through some of the armour. Not waiting for the Forester to counter, he followed up with a series of accurate and deadly slashes aimed at gaps between the carapace. The Forester's song stopped abruptly. Sabretooth shook his arms in the air in triumph turning to look at the Wastelanders who roared in excitement to see the Forester struggling to stand.

Gladerwin staggered back, his eyes widening in utter shock, as he looked down to see dark red trickling from cuts all over. His survival instincts kicked in, anger, fear and adrenalin fuelled him to remain standing and fight.

Grasping his great sword with the last of his strength he swung it high above his head, bringing it down with surprising agility and speed for someone so large.

The sword flew through the air clumsily, but striking the pirate captain with such force, that the crude pirate armour offered little to no protection. Rage running through his blood, Gladerwin swung again, his sword delivering another deadly blow. The pirate crumpled to the ground, unconscious, to a roaring song from the Virdarians.

Gladerwin staggered back another step, trying to compose himself, as the impact had further opened up the wounds on his body. The trickles of blood now became gushes. He dropped the heavy sword, overcome by a wave of dizziness, and tried to steady himself as he stumbled onto his knees.

He opened his mouth as if to speak something, then dropped backwards onto the dusty sandy ground. The wind lashed up the sand as though in response to the sudden outbreak of rage. And soon, the two bodies of both mortally wounded men began to get covered by sand making their way to becoming part of those looming dunes.

Hundreds of eyes looked on in horror. And at that, the two sides lost the last of their rational thoughts and had only blood on their minds. At once a gigantic rumbling song boomed across the desert as the Virdarians sang together in unison, their eyes filled with rage. They raised their ancient weapons and charged down towards their fallen leader with great leaping bounds. The Wastelanders narrowed their eyes, raised their swords, and gave an equally terrifying call. They rushed forwards, a great wave of writhing, seething bodies, down the gangplanks and onto the soft dunes.

CHAPTER TWENTY TWO

Moments before the great and bloody clash, a tiny lone ship whizzed across the sandy seas, barely touching the ground as it darted over dune after dune, and through winding valleys of sand.

'We've got to make it in time!' Der called out with razor-like urgency. They tensed their bodies, holding on tightly as they skipped across the bumpy surface. Their eyes remained fixed on the lines and shapes displayed on the night-vision screen, guiding the ship as it flew like a bat through the darkness.

'Hang on, what's that?' Skoots yelled, pointing to a patch of heat-signatures on the infrared screen.

'And that?' Der replied. Soon their screen was filled with heat-signatures up ahead. But by then, it was not the screen that alarmed them, it was the ever-increasing roaring, blood curdling scream that came from ahead.

They were rapidly approaching the middle of the

oncoming battle, as on both sides a boiling mass of bodies descended from the dunes. With hands as steady as the rocks, Der angled the prow of the ship towards the ever-narrowing void between the approaching armies. Her hands went taut as she braced herself.

Skoot's face was gripped by a look of utter fear. His eyes widened, his mouth fell into a gawping tunnel and he let out a cry. 'No, Der! Turn us around!'

But his words were swallowed up by the wails and screams of the battle cries and the roaring of the ship as it smashed through the air and sand like a rocket towards the closing gap.

Der closed her eyes, readying herself, knowing that they would probably be consumed by both violent waves, but secretly hoping that somehow or another she could get their attention and shout 'Stop!'. It was a fool's plan. Brave and honourable, but a fool's plan.

Skoots tensed for impact as the metres dropped. Twenty-five. Twenty-four. He half closed his eyes, part of him wanting to not see, the other needing to see. Twenty. Nineteen. Der tensed her body even more, causing the seat to creak and groan.

Sixteen. Fifteen. Fourteen. Tears, not of sadness but of fear, trickled down Skoot's face and his hands shook. Ten. Nine. Then with a quick glance at his BFF, Skoots grabbed the wheel and with a vicious yank swung the ship around, steering away from the collision course with such velocity that the whole vehicle lurched to one side.

It teetered for a blink of an eye before completely flipping over, the mast cracking and splintering into shards. The sheer force of inertia catapulted the ship across the sand, throwing Der and Skoots violently from the wreckage, as a cloud of dust billowed out, obscuring the carnage of the ship and its contents.

Der opened her eyes, a sharp pain stretching down her leg, and her head aching and hazy. She squinted to see through the sandy cloud, trying to piece together how she came to be lying hurt on the side of a dune.

A groan came from beside her. She slowly shifted her aching head around to see Skoots. He was alive but clutching his arm. At last Der managed to piece together the memories of what had taken place; the harrowing war cries that had sent shivers down her spine. But something was odd now, there was a disturbing silence, that had momentarily washed over the whole dune.

The sandy clouds cleared to reveal two massive armies standing perplexed, squinting down at the tiny twisted ship and the two small figures on the dune bank.

They had stopped mid-charge, weapons in their hands tensed ready to clash. Der hobbled to her feet, crying out in pain, a trickle of blood running down her cheek from a gash on her head. Her vision was blurred and time seemed to slow down into one long second. But a second… a second is sometimes all it takes, to bring down a city, smash a dream, break a heart, or walk away forever. But it is also, sometimes, all it takes to save a life, send a smile, forgive a deed, change a heart, or even change the course of everything! And in that tiny drop of time in a vast and immeasurable ocean, Der let out a cry.

It was not a cry of pain, or sadness, but a cry of desperation. A cry from the very depths of her heart, that cut through the clouded minds on that battlefield just for a second. Her voice carried on the wind, like a bird, keen and shrill: 'STOP!'

She lurched forward, swaying, towards the statue-like figures, fighting with her cloudy vision to keep walking.

'Stop! Please, I beg you. Don't do this. You're better than this. Please at least stop and hear me out!' she cried in a desperate and cracking voice as tears trickled down her face, at the sight of the two groups she had grown to love.

Eyes from both sides met each other. Not a word was spoken, but in those eyes a thousand words passed. Little by little, their grips on their weapons began to relax, mirroring each other tentatively.

Der continued in a clear and urgent tone. 'Please listen to what I have to say, we don't have much time.' She grasped her pounding head. 'There are winds coming, so powerful that they could tear the forest apart, and so much rainwater that it will flood all of Balldock. If you don't put aside your differences and work quickly to evacuate, you will all die!'

Her words rang through the silent statues' ears. Puzzled looks and gasps washed over each face, as they tried to understand what she had just said.

A short, robust shipwright stepped forward, a large wooden mallet in his hand. 'And how do you know that wind and water will come?' he growled.

A tall figure joined him. 'Yeah, and how do you know it will be that dangerous? We haven't had wind or water like that for generations.'

Suddenly Skoots was standing at her side swaying, his arm trickling with blood, seemingly broken. 'I know we haven't. But you have to trust us, or you will all perish here!' he shouted.

Der noticed the looks of bewilderment on the Virdarian faces and she searched her hazy mind, trying to remember some fragments of Virdarian that Golderwin had taught her. She took a deep breath. 'Wind destroy forest forever,' she sang.

One of the Virdarians that thought he understood Der's words stepped forward, his bearded and rugged face a wash of emotion. He opened his mouth wide and let out a short melodic song.

'How do you know the wind can destroy our forest?' he sang. 'It has stood for generations, if not forever.' But sadly the Wastelanders were not even slightly accustomed with the Foresters' song.

'Oy, they're mocking us again. They just want war!' Scarlan snarled, seizing her chance to take control. A disgruntled mumble of contempt began to bubble up from the Wastelanders' ranks, like a kettle on a low boil.

Der narrowed her eyes, shifted her wounded leg and

shouted with a look of determination. 'Wait! No, the Forester isn't mocking you at all. They don't speak like us to communicate, they use song.' She panted, trying to catch her breath. It was hard work just standing, let alone trying to speak. Skoots tried to steady her, putting his one good arm around her for support.

'What did the Forester say then, girl?' Scarlan asked mockingly.

But she didn't have a chance to answer, because a familiar voice rang out from behind the Virdarian ranks. 'The Forester asked how she knows that the winds can destroy our forest,' the voice boomed, as the speaker dashed in, half out of breath. He was unarmoured, with a simple waistcoat and a long cloak that billowed out like a small sail in the gusting wind.

'Golderwin!' Der gasped.

His eyes were still red with tears and his limbs were weary from having run so far from the Forest, but he turned to face Der with a warm look in his eyes. She smiled and unspoken words passed between them.

'How do you know all this, Derwin?' Golderwin asked.

'I know these things because we found an ancient station in the desert, designed to measure information about the wind and rain. And it predicted that there's a mega-storm coming.'

Her answer was met by a barrage of questions. 'Where is this place?' a pirate voice shot in.

And another, 'What is a mega-storm?'. The

questions came thick and fast, far too many for Der to even begin to answer.

Scarlan stepped forward and spoke in a fierce voice. 'We came here for war, to avenge our pirate kind killed by you,' she sneered, pointing a finger at the Virdarians, 'not to listen to some girl. I say we tell these kids to stand over there while we teach these Foresters a lesson or two.'

This was met by equal uproar from the Virdarians, as the kettle of rage began to bubble and boil again.

Suddenly a stern voice cut through the mob. 'Silence! On behalf of all the Wastelanders, I demand you hear this girl!' And there, on the prow of his newly arrived ship, stood Silvaran, his one good eye glinting in the moonlight and his sword drawn.

At his side stood Arc, her eyes glaring like fire. Grogen towered beside her, gripping his sword. Behind them were eight young Virdarians, their heads hung in sombre tears. Skoots limped over and hugged his sister, happy she was still alive.

Golderwin turned to his people. 'I vouch for this girl; let her speak. Our forest may well depend on it.' His song was met by nods of agreement. 'Derwin, my people will hear you,' he said, turning back to her. The two great armies now stood resolutely, listening as Der continued.

'In not much more than a few hours, there will be no Forest or Balldock to fight over and you will all die here, even if you survive each other's swords. How about you all trust me, for a few hours at least? If I'm wrong, you can always come back tomorrow with even more weapons, and kill each other then.' She looked from side to side in desperation.

'But if I'm right, we will save everyone here, and your children and families back home, from the most terrible storm in centuries. We don't have much time.'

Golderwin's low and melancholy song was met by a chorus of replies from his people. The Virdarians nodded to one another and began to sheathe their swords and strap their spears to their backs.

'They agree to let you have sunrise and sunset, to prove this,' Golderwin announced with a triumphant smile. 'They will follow your command until this time tomorrow.'

Der turned to the motley crew of Wastelanders, her eyebrow raised in anticipation. Scarlan stepped forward, the gouge of her old scar glistening in the moonlight.

'Silvaran! You think you can roll up here and demand we listen to you and this girl? Take a look around, your crew are long gone. Only your retired sidekick and your pet remain!'

Arc took a step forward, her sword drawn and eyes aflame, while Grogen's face twisted into a seething look of anger. Silvaran remained calm, as she continued.

'You might have once been a legend, old man, but those days have long gone! Take a look around. Me and my friends here outnumber you by hundreds, and your authority is no more. I'm not afraid of a bit of water and wind. Hey, it will help to wash the blood away after we take down these Foresters and your sorry hide, Silvaran. Who is with me?' she boomed, and a blazing roar went up among the pirates.

'But you will all die in the storm!' Der protested.

'Not us. We are not afraid of a bit a water and wind, are we?' She was met by a rumbling chorus of laughter from her crew. Silvaran glanced at Der and shook his head.

Just then Der had an idea. 'Well it's up to you, but the Fulgur will be here soon.' Silence swept across the pirates as a wave of fear washed over them.

'Fulgur? Where? When?' they murmured.

'Coming from over there, very soon!' Der said defiantly. 'But I'm leaving with the Foresters and Silvaran here before it comes.'

Then in a strange and unbefitting tone a lone voice called out from the back, 'Take us with you! We don't want to face the Fulgur.' Bit by bit, more voices joined in, as the air filled with the sound of swords being sheathed. Der winked at Silvaran and bowed respectfully towards both the Wastelanders and Virdarians. When she spoke next, she spoke calmly but briskly.

'Right, we must get everyone out of Balldock and the Forest, and travel east as quickly as possible. There's an old cave network that's far enough from the path of old Fulgur the mega-storm, and strong enough to withstand it. Everyone, meet me here as soon as you've gathered your people. We need to travel light, so leave your weapons, and only bring food and water. Enough for as long as possible!'

At that, the great hordes hurried off in different directions to evacuate their people. But just before Golderwin turned to leave, two eyes met his. One of the young Virdarians that Silvaran had freed from the Cockroaches ran towards Golderwin, and the two embraced. 'Arberwin, I thought I would never see you again,' Golderwin sobbed.

'And Mum?' Arberwin asked. A silence fell between them and tears of sadness flooded their eyes. At last they turned and began the steady march back towards the Forest.

***

Satisa stood proud upon the bow of her ship, her sword drawn. 'Where is that wretched ally of ours? Maybe she didn't make it out alive?' she muttered to herself. 'That should be long enough, surely, we can't wait for her word.' Turning to the other three ships, 'Let's sail out and finish them all!' she roared.

Four ships rumbled forward from the edge of the forest, sailing double time, out into the blustery dunes.

'Captain, ship approaching on the horizon!' a call went up from the mast.

'What flag are they flying, friend or foe?' Satisa screamed.

'Looks like Captain Scarlan,' announced the lookout. A whistle went up and the four ships changed course, hurtling towards the lone craft on the horizon, the wind lashing around them as they went.

***

The journey to the caves had been stressful and panicked as the first sign of the storm, or Fulgur as they imagined it, had swept in. They had only just made it as the first few pools of water had plopped onto the arid ground and the air was filled with that fresh sweet smell of rain.

Just after the last of them had hurried through the twisting tunnels a little way up the cliffside, the first rumbles of thunder echoed in the distance and even after everyone had safely hunkered down in the caves, they could hear the wind whipping up into a frenzy.

Both Virdarians and Aridians sat together in silence, clutching their children and the few sacks of food and water they had been able to carry in the flight from their homes. Their hearts were filled with fear, but also gratitude.

The seven freed Virdarian slaves milled around looking for villagers they recognised, and one by one were reunited with their long lost families in tearful embraces.

'Is that the last of our people, old friend?' Golderwin called.

'I think so,' replied Silvaran. 'That was close, but thanks to Der and Skoots here we are safe.'

Der and Skoots mustered a smile. They were sitting close together and resting their injuries, holding hands for comfort.

Golderwin stepped towards Silvaran and dropped down to his knees, suddenly overwhelmed with tears.

'You saved my son. He told me the whole story,' he howled, pointing to Arberwin. 'Silvaran, how can I ever repay you? I thought he was lost forever. Like my poor Flosorwin.'

'There is nothing to repay. Knowing he is safe is enough,' Silvaran replied. 'Our people aren't so different you know, old friend. There is far more that unites us than divides us. Now get up and stand tall next to me. Our people need us.'

Golderwin stood up and the two age-old friends embraced. Then with determination in their eyes, they gave orders ensuring everyone had water and food.

Gladerwin's wife – Brookorwin – sat alone, her eyes red with tears. 'Would you like some water?' Grogen offered, his voice uncharacteristically soft. Their eyes met and an understanding beyond words passed in their glance. They sat together for a while, both in silence, but slightly less alone.

Suddenly great angry howls rumbled through the cave, louder and louder as the wind hurtled around the flat desert lands and smashed against the rocks outside. The horrifying sounds frightened both the toughest of pirates and Foresters alike.

Noticing that even Golderwin was afraid, Silvaran was at his side. 'Remember the song we used to sing together so long ago, old friend,' Silvaran said. 'Round those evening campfires on the fringe of both of our worlds, when we were so young and loved to talk and sing the nights away.'

A strange booming song rumbled from the depths of Golderwin in reply, a concoction of both Virdarian and Aridian. The melody bounced around the dim walls of the cave, picking up speed. It was soon joined by Silvaran's voice, singing in perfect unison. Their people listened, intrigued, the beautiful and catchy tunes getting under their skin, till one by one they began to join in.

Soon the wind and rain were joined by flashes of lightning so intense that the light charged down the tunnels and even into the caves themselves, evaporating the shadows. The cave trembled with the violent crashes from outside. But as they sat through it all, the louder the storm raged the louder they all sang in unity, as if to drown out the fury of the storm. The minutes turned to hours and hours turned into days. No one knew quite how long it was till the storm began to simmer down, but eventually it did, leaving an eerie silence from outside.

When they eventually emerged like waking animals from hibernation, the whole landscape looked different. Lit by the silver moon in a crystal-clear sky, the dunes had been flattened and dispersed, while rocks and boulders lay strewn everywhere, having fallen from the very cliff face that had housed them in safety.

The armada of ships that they had used to sail to the caves were nowhere to be seen. They had been smashed and flung around so violently, that only matchstick sized pieces could be found nestling in the sand.

EPILOGUE

'Is that where your dream finished, Grandma?'

'Dream? I… I…' the frail old lady stuttered, trying to make sense of her clouded mind and separate dreams from memory.

The fire had burnt down to the last glowing embers, and the orange glow danced over her granddaughter Gelwin's face as she clutched her small book and pencil. She looked up, another question burning in her mind.

'Gran, so what happened to the Virdarians and the Wastelanders?'

The old lady brushed her hair out of her eyes, as she tried to remember the next part of the story.

'Well, Gelwin dear. It was terrible, but in the sadness of having lost their homes, the Virdarians and Wastelanders eventually found common ground, and those first seeds of friendship blossomed in time. Der, Skoots and Golderwin – well, they became trusted by all, and formed the "Forest Alliance" uniting the Wastelanders and Virdarians. They even began to learn each other's languages.'

Gelwin sketched away in the dying firelight, still listening intently. Then looking back up again she said,

‘And what of the Last Forest, Gran? Was that the end of it forever?’

‘No, dear. Skoots and Der managed to build another ship and sailed back to the weather station to research more about weather patterns and reforestation. Golderwin’s tree survived and safely below it in the cavern were his people’s seed stores. Golderwin and his son Arberwin took charge of cleaning up the forest and showed everyone how to plant the seeds and tend to the saplings. Silvaran and Grogen returned to Fringetown, to gather electronics requested by Der. And Arc trained a team of people to patrol and protect the forest.

Soon, the first trees sprouted, and with the care and love of the Virdarians, and clever use of the Wastelanders’ technology, the forest became green again. In time, three guilds were established. The knights to protect the newly grown Forest, led by the formidable Arc. The Gardeners to tend to the Forest, led by Golderwin and Arberwin. And the Tech-keepers led by Der and Skoots, to build ships, predict the weather, and generate energy for all. Der even set up a school using some of the books from the weather centre. And now the Forest stretches further than it has done for centuries!’ the old lady said with a look of triumph as she glanced out of the window.

‘And what about Der and Skoots, was that the last of their adventures?’

‘No, dear. They built another stealth ship and between their times helping the Forest Alliance, they had many more adventures, exploring far and distant lands, discovering other groups of people, and all sorts of wonderful places. And eventually they settled down together.'

Gelwin continued to sketch away diligently in her book. Then her eyes wandered around the small room as the soft evening shadows played with the sparse objects on the walls and tables, till her eyes rested back on her grandma. Just then a soft voice called up to the young girl from the front door downstairs. 'It's time to go home, darling.'

Gelwin kissed her grandma and whispered, 'Give my love to Grandad when he wakes up.'

Then she sped off downstairs where she was met by an exceptionally tall lady with long brown hair and rather large ears.

'Hi Aunt Leawin,' she said cheerfully.

'How were Gran and Grandad today, dear?' she asked as they ambled down the forest path.

'Grandad was asleep, but Gran was awake and told me a story about her dream. There was a girl called Der that saved the Forest from a storm and a war.'

Her aunt looked strangely amused, 'Ah, I know that story too, dear, but it wasn't a dream, it really happened. Your gran and grandad really did save the Forest and its people from a war. But that was a long time ago. You might even learn about it at school when you are older. Sadly, your grandma gets confused nowadays and even forgets her own name.'

'She spoke about going to school in the oldie world. Is that bit true too?' the little girl asked expectantly.

Leawin chuckled. 'No, sadly that's just a silly dream. She has always had odd dreams, your gran.'

The girl looked up at the evening stars twinkling through the vast forest canopy and the shimmering silver of the two moons, as the story coursed through her vivid memory and filled her with excitement. An idea sparked in her mind.

'Hang on, I forgot something, Aunt. I'll be right back!' she said as she sped off back into the house and up the stairs.

'Gran, wake up!' she said loudly.

'Huh?' the old lady said, waking suddenly.

'Gran, this is for you!' she whispered, holding out her book of drawings and smiling. 'So, you don't ever forget that you are Der again!'

Gelwin rushed back downstairs as quickly as she had come, but the old lady barely noticed, as the words 'You are Der' reverberated in her mind. It seemed to stir deep memories and she wrestled to unravel the broken shards. She glanced at the small book her granddaughter had given her and opened it.

A smile swept across her face as she flicked through the lovingly drawn pages, till suddenly she came to a sketch of an old bracelet. With a frown of confusion, she held up her wrist to reveal, nestled between wrinkles, an old and quite nondescript bracelet, with four shapes.

Shapes that felt important.

A moment of clarity came over her. 'I *am* Der!' she declared in a loud voice. She inspected the bracelet, holding her wrist inches from her half-blind eyes.

'Yes, *I am Der*! I remember now!' she shouted.

She stood up abruptly and staggered across the room, throwing open the adjoining door and startling an old man who had been asleep in bed.

'Hey, wake up! I am Der!'

The old man came to and gently said, 'Calm down, my dear Der. You have forgotten again, that's all.'

'I remember your name too,' she replied. 'You are Skoots.'

'Oh, my dear Der. Have you had that dream again?'

Der stared deep into the old man's eyes. 'No. I mean yes, but it isn't a dream. It's real, and I'm not from this world!' she said.

'It's just a crazy dream, old girl. We had some good adventures, but none ever to the land of oldies! Those times were centuries ago, long before our time.'

'It is true and not a dream, you old fool. I'm telling the truth, I remember now. Come with me, Skoots, I'll show you, take my hand.'

Skoots looked deeply into her sparkling eyes, strangely the only thing still the same since that first day they had met in Fringetown. He placed his hand in hers and laughed.

'OK my BFF,' he said, humouring her. 'One more adventure for the road; I will be your ride or die!'

She reached over and touched the four shapes on her old bracelet: a circle, a star, a square, then a hexagon. And the room faded away to black.

She was falling through the void, streams of coloured light flashing by, before coming to a sudden halt on a hard wooden floor.

Der looked around. She was back in her bedroom, the bedroom she thought was from her dream. And in her hand was a small child's toy with shapes on it.

'It was only a dream,' she declared. 'The Forest, the desert, the war. Wow, what a dream!' She glanced at the clock on her desk, and it read 11:00. Then from behind her there was a groan and rustle.

'Der. Where am I?' a stressed voice said. She spun round to see Skoots standing there before her with a look of cloudy confusion on his face.

'I remember your name is Der. But where are we? I… I… can't remember much about my life before now,' Skoots said, his memories becoming foggy.

Der could remember a bit. She was trying to hold on to the fragments of their life together, but she too could feel it slipping away like grains of sand through her fingers.

They both stood staring at each other. Smile lines and wrinkles filled their faces, carved by the chisels of time. As Der moved to touch Skoot's face, she paused, remembering the book in her pocket. She opened it carefully and as they both stood gazing at the drawings, memories cascaded back through the desert of their minds like a raging waterfall. They remembered it all.

'Oh, my dear Skoots. I told you we had one last adventure in us! I told you this place wasn't just a dream!' Der exclaimed.

Skoots was feeling exhausted from the journey and the memory loss. He sat on the floor and mumbled, 'Sadly, my dear, I think this is the end of our adventures; we are so very old now. What a life we led together.'

But suddenly Der remembered something. A dream. Or perhaps not. A dream of a strange place where time was even stranger, a place where time ran backwards.

'Could we live our lives backwards and become young again?' she pondered.

Before Skoots could object, she had grabbed his hand, and was punching in four shapes on the toy. At once the room faded and they were swept away, still holding hands, streams of coloured light dazzling them as they tumbled through the void.

ACKNOWLEDGEMENTS

Developmental Editor – I would like to thank Thomas Dalton for his support throughout the whole process. For pushing and challenging me to keep evolving and improving the plot and characters.

Proofreader & Copy-editor – I would like to thank Helen Baggott for her attention to detail, professional advice and guidance.

Beta Readers – I would like to thank the following Beta readers, for taking time to read the book and for their constructive, kind and supportive comments:
Rev Andy Bawtree
Gillian Rowland
Thomas Dalton
Nettie Brannon
Daisy-B (age 11)

Publisher – I would like to thank my publisher, Louannvee, and in particular Nettie for all her time and attention. Could not have done it without you!

The Last Forest – Designed and made by Alexander Way-B.

Graphic design advice – A big thank you to Alexandre M, an exceptionally talented graphic designer, for all his professional advice and support.

Font for Blurb:

A big thank you to Typodermic Fonts for allowing us to use their font Good Timing. They have designed some very beautiful fonts.

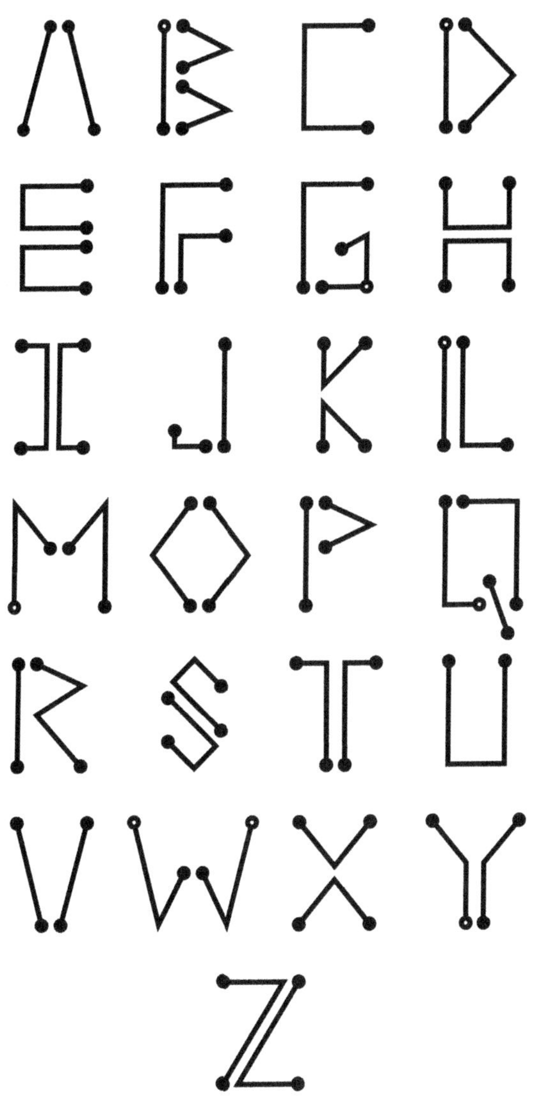

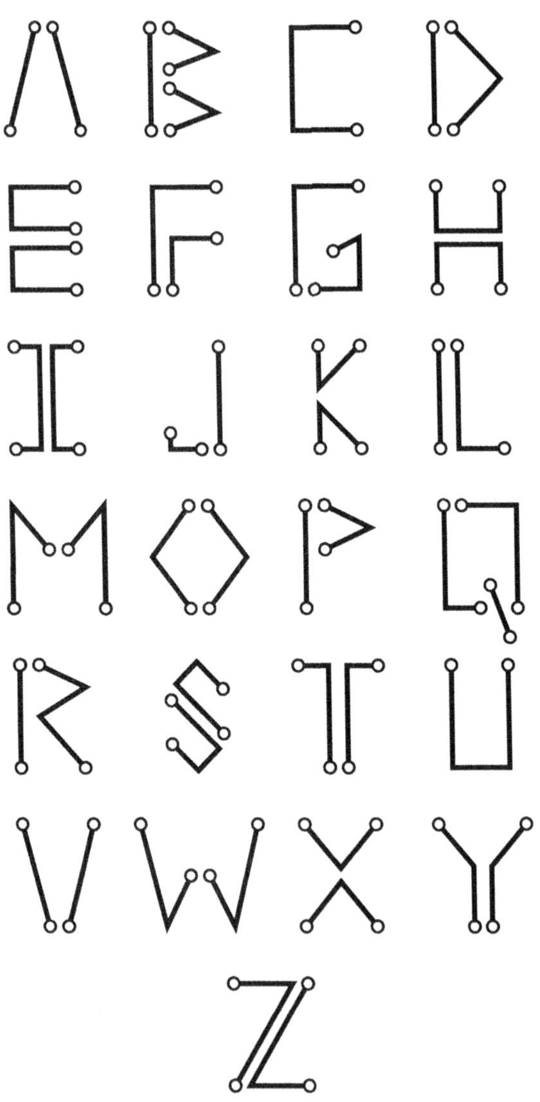

If you've enjoyed sharing Der's first adventure in

The Last Forest

Please write a review
Thank you

www.louannveepublishing.co.uk

Printed in Great Britain
by Amazon

18168787R00171